IN THE ANCIENT SANDS OF THE MIDDLE EAST, MURDER AND GREED GUARD THE WORLD'S MOST MAGICAL TREASURE. . . .

INDIANA JONES—He survived a trap-laden Chinese tomb, crossed the Himalayas and a land aflame with war to help a woman in distress and to locate a biblical artifact and the priceless, dangerous treasure it will unlock.

MASTER SOKAI—A Japanese spymaster of Bushido, the way of the warrior, he was once gravely wounded by Indiana Jones. Now he lives for one purpose: to track down the famous explorer and exact his revenge.

FAYE MASKELYNE—The beautiful American granddaughter of a famous English magician, she is a sorceress in her own right, searching for her child's missing father. But her illusions prove useless in her search until she conjures up the aid of a man named Indy.

JADOO—In the East, his name itself means magic. The most famous conjurer in the Orient, he claims to be 123 years old—but his lust for life is only exceeded by his thirst for evil . . . and his desire to possess the most powerful magical object of all.

THE STAFF OF AARON—In the Bible it turned into a snake, made the Nile run with blood, and blossomed into an almond tree in the Wilderness. Now the Staff of Aaron will lead to the Egyptian desert—and the most dangerous wonder of the world.

THE INDIANA JONES SERIES
Ask your bookseller for the books you have missed

AND THE

SECRET OF
THE SPHINX

MAX McCOY

BANTAM BOOKS
NEW YORK   TORONTO   LONDON   SYDNEY   AUCKLAND

INDIANA JONES AND THE SECRET OF THE SPHINX
A Bantam Book

PUBLISHING HISTORY
Bantam mass market edition published February 1999
Bantam reissue / April 2008

Published by
Bantam Dell
A Division of Random House, Inc.
New York, New York

ISBN 978-0-553-56197-5

Printed in the United States of America
Published simultaneously in Canada

www.bantamdell.com

OPM   13 12 11 10 9 8 7 6 5

For Mystery,
wherever you may find her

Aaron cast down his rod before Pharaoh, and before his servants, and it became a serpent. . . . Now the magicians of Egypt, they also did in like manner with their enchantments. . . . But Aaron's rod swallowed up their rods.

—*Exodus*, 7:10–12

AND THE

SECRET OF
THE SPHINX

1

THE TOMB OF TERROR

Mount Hua, Shaanxi Province, China—1934

"The door," the villager croaked and rapped the side of the Sacred Mountain with his walking stick. "I leave now."

"No," Indiana Jones said as he batted dust from his fedora and struggled to catch his breath. The climb had been tougher than it had looked at dusk from the bottom of the mountain. Now half the night was gone and there was still much to be done. "The deal was to take me back down the mountain as well," Indy said as he placed his hands on his knees and leaned forward to ease the pain in his chest. "Or don't you think I'm coming back?"

The old villager smiled serenely. He hugged his

walking stick and regarded the gasping American through milky eyes. Then he gave a lazy smile that revealed a mouthful of jagged teeth as he leaned forward.

"Jones pay Lo now," he said.

Indy gritted his teeth.

Looking at Lo's face from this distance reminded Indy of holding a pet rat and peering down its grinning snout—you didn't know when the rat was going to sink his teeth into your fingers, you just knew that eventually it would.

Lo was the best guide in the province, but he was the most notorious liar as well. When Indy first came to the village of Lintong, three days ago, Lo had bragged that he had been inside all of the important treasure tombs of the Wei Bei Plain. And although Lo could name the occupants of each of the tombs and describe in blood-curdling detail what horrors lurked in each, Indy knew it had been a long time since the villager had seen the interior of an unlooted grave, if indeed he ever had; otherwise, he wouldn't have found him living on top of a garbage mound, begging foreigners for money to buy opium.

"I don't see any door here," Indy said.

Indy took a rag from his back pocket and wiped the blood from his palms, injured from scrabbling for holds in the face of the mountain. His elbows and shins ached from several near-falls, and the muscles in his lower back quivered like rubber.

"Door there," Lo said. "Feel."

As Indy's fingertips touched the outlines of what did appear to be a doorway, his cuts and bruises were forgotten. His hands skittered over the granite like curious spiders, tracing a perfect circle about a yardstick in diameter as they followed the edges of the door, then moved inward. When his right hand came to a stone handle carved in the middle of the door, his fingers closed tightly around it.

He gave a tug.

It felt as solid as the mountain to which it was attached.

Lo giggled. The villager continued to chortle as he covered his mouth with his left hand, and eventually it became an insulting, lilting laugh.

"Told you," Lo said. "It cannot be opened. Some say it takes the right kind of magic, others say that the door is just picture carved into the mountain."

"What do you say?" Indy asked.

"I tell you when I get my money."

"All right," Indy said. As he counted out a fistful of bills of various countries and denominations from the pockets of his leather jacket, he asked Lo: "Why aren't you tired? I'm tired."

"Americans breathe too shallow, always out of air," Lo said and made an elaborate gesture with his hands of air flowing in and then out of his diaphragm. "Must breathe all the way to stomach and feed chi, the life force."

Indy shook his head.

"You're not so bad for an opium addict," he said as he thrust out the bills.

Lo snatched the colorful wad of money out of Indy's hand, counted it, then tucked it inside his sash. "Not always addict," Lo said. "Once best damn grave robber in mausoleum district. Then the Japanese come."

Lo spat.

"Now, no way for Lo to make honest living."

Since the Imperial Japanese Army had seized Manchuria, raiding parties had been crossing the border with some regularity and searching for plunder in the fabled mausoleum district. The district contained the tombs of eleven dynasties of Chinese royalty, and lay just north of the provincial capital of Xi'an—or Changan, as it was called in ancient times—the "City of Everlasting Peace" at the end of the Silk Road. Bristling over the plain like a dragon protecting her lair was the jagged outline of Mount Hua, the Sacred Mountain.

All of the easy tombs had long ago been plundered; for most, it was just a matter of digging into the conspicuous-looking mounds the locals called "lings." Still, Indy believed, there must be some that were beyond the reach of a shovel. Beneath the river, perhaps, or inside the mountain.

Indy was counting on the latter.

Besides, it wasn't all guesswork on Indy's part. He had been guided here by the inscription on the blade of a knife which said the Sacred Mountain was the tomb of Qin Shi Huang, first emperor of China. The knife had been given to Indy by a descendant of Genghis Khan during an expedition across the Gobi.

"The Japanese raiders will be back at first light, so we'd better work fast," Indy said. "Tell me about this door."

"Just picture carved into mountain," Lo said arrogantly. "Once, seventeen years ago, Lo and his cousins came to this spot and tied a thick rope around the handle. Then we put a log over boulder there, tied rope to end of it, and all pushed on end of log."

"What happened?"

"Rope broke," Lo said and turned to leave. "Good-bye."

"Not quite yet," Indy said as he smoothly placed the fedora on his head, then grabbed the villager's shoulder with the same hand.

"What else to do?" Lo asked.

"Research," Indy said as he took his notebook out of his satchel. He held the pencil in his mouth as he flipped to a page marked by a rubber band. There was a sketch of a round door, along with its dimensions, that Indy had copied from an ancient Arab manuscript. The manuscript was unrelated to the Qin treasure, but Indy had discovered that the architects of secret places thought alike, even if they were from different centuries and cultures. The tip-off for Indy was the last line of the inscription on the knife blade: *The breath of the Sacred Mountain protects the tomb of Qin.*

Indy now had a tape and was comparing the measurements of the door with those of the sketch. When he was satisfied, he took a piece of chalk from his satchel and, measuring carefully from a small indentation in the center of the handle, made an X on the right half of the door. Then he took a metal protractor, measured the angle from the edge of the tape, and made another X at the same distance, but forty-five degrees from the line of the first. Finally Indy measured the distance, halved it, and placed a larger X between the original marks.

"Qin, old man," Indy said. "X marks the spot."

"What kind of magic is this?" Lo asked.

"Geometry," Indy said as he replaced the chalk and notebook and removed a rock hammer and a chisel from the satchel. The chisel was tapered to a sharp, needlelike point.

"Now, I'm going to make some noise. It

shouldn't take long, but it could attract some unwanted attention. Keep a sharp eye out."

Lo nodded.

Indy placed the tip of the chisel against the chalk mark, drew back the rock hammer, then struck the butt of the chisel hard enough that sparks flew.

Lo covered his ears against the clanging sound.

Indy continued to hammer, quicker and with more vigor, turning the chisel as he went. More sparks and bits of granite erupted from the point of the chisel.

He stopped after a dozen blows, blew away the rock dust, and inspected the depression he was making in the stone door. "Maybe I've got the wrong spot, but from the book I found in Cairo—" Indy gritted his teeth. "No, this is it. I haven't made a mistake."

Indy placed the chisel firmly against the spot, drew the hammer back, and struck. The chisel broke through—accompanied by a sound like a rifle shot—then disappeared from Indy's hand as it was snatched through the door by some unseen power.

Lo placed a hand to his mouth and stepped back.

There was a whistling sound as a torrent of night air was sucked in through the hole. Within seconds, the surface of the door around the hole was coated with a white layer of frost that was quickly turning to ice.

"Black magic," Lo stuttered.

"Not quite," Indy said when the rush of air had subsided. Indy grasped the handle and pulled. The round door, which fit like a tapered cork into the pipelike tunnel behind it, began to come forward. Lo rushed to help Indy with the door, and soon the three-hundred-pound cork was resting between them.

"But how?" Lo asked.

"Vacuum," Indy said. "The tomb had been sealed with a partial vacuum. Just a slight difference in air pressure makes locks and chains unnecessary. You found out that a team of horses couldn't have pulled that door away. But break the seal and equalize the pressure, and it becomes rather simple."

Lo nodded.

"The chisel broke through the mortared-over holes where the tomb builders stuck their hoses to pump the air out," Indy said as he brought out a battery-powered light. He strapped the lamp and reflector over his fedora and clipped the battery pack to his belt. To keep the power cord out of his face, he ran it through a belt loop over his back pocket before plugging it in.

"What Jones think is inside?" Lo asked, his eyes gleaming. "The stories I have heard since childhood—mountains of gold, rivers of silver, a skyful of jewels."

"I intend to find out," Indy said as he climbed into the tunnel. Then he shot Lo a stern look. "I will assume anybody else in there with me means trouble—and act accordingly." Indy rested his right hand on the holstered butt of his .38-caliber revolver. "If I find anybody else in there with me—well, anybody else who hasn't been dead for a few thousand years—I will shoot them. Do you understand?"

Lo nodded.

"Good," Indy said. "Stay here and stand guard. If there's any trouble, give a shout. If I'm not back in an hour before first light, leave."

Indy looked at his watch. It was past one o'clock in the morning. Then he took a gulp of fresh night air and ducked into the tunnel. It soon opened onto a wide corridor with stairs spiraling downward. The vaulted ceiling was high enough for Indy to stand without worrying about crushing the crown of his hat, and the corridor seemed unthreatening until Indy completed the first revolution of the downward spiral.

He was greeted by the first of what would become a seemingly endless row of terra-cotta soldiers lining the sides of the tunnel, standing at the ready, their faces frozen forever in menace. Their eyes were polished stones of blue, red, and green, which had been set into the clay before it dried. Their cheeks bulged out, as if they were preparing to blow up an ancient balloon, and their lips formed delicate O's, and behind many of these lips were the same kinds of marbles as the eyes. Up from the floor ran a stout piece of bamboo that, Indy supposed, helped keep the statues upright. Even their balance was artificial, Indy thought; the only real things about the soldiers, it seemed, were their weapons: Swords gleamed, lances threatened, and crossbows remained cocked and pointed at the center of the passage.

Indy particularly disliked the look of the crossbows.

He noticed that no two of the soldiers were alike, despite the similarities of marble eyes and bulbous cheeks. It wasn't just that they were in different poses or had different weapons or clothes; each figure had its own face, its own personality, as if the sculptor had taken his inspiration for each face from life, but had transformed the original visage into a grotesque parody.

A few yards farther on, Indy found his chisel on the floor of the tunnel amid some brown shards. He knelt, put the chisel back in his satchel, then stood to inspect the clay soldier his unintended missile had struck.

The victim had fallen against a comrade to the right. The chisel had struck the soldier beneath his sword arm, shattering the clay armor over his rib cage. Indy directed the light into the hole.

Inside, human bones shone like ivory.

Indy knew of the folktales about Qin, first emperor of China and architect of the Great Wall, who ruled two hundred years before the birth of Christ. According to legend, it had taken seven hundred thousand laborers nearly four decades to build his tomb (which, according to legend, was a miniature replica of the universe) and two hundred thousand of his best troops had been buried with him. It was not uncommon for kings to be interred with guards, servants, or family members to make their afterlife more pleasant, but Indy had doubted the size of Qin's spirit army. Now, walking between the rows of terra-cotta corpses, he was not so sure. The soldiers looked as if they were ready to spring to life to protect Qin's treasure.

Since the tomb had been hermetically sealed, not even a layer of dust coated the terra-cotta army. The floor and the walls of the corridor were as unstained if they had been constructed yesterday. Indy had the uncomfortable feeling that he had broken in to a modern, well-designed museum, rather than a tomb that had lain undisturbed for thousands of years.

Anxious to be out of the tomb by daylight, Indy pressed on.

He almost did not feel the silken thread against

his face or notice the crossbow, held in lifeless hands, that was pointed at him. But reflexes took over as he felt the thread part over the bridge of his nose, and finally noticed the gleaming head of the crossbow bolt aimed at his solar plexus.

The bowstring twanged, but Indy was already doing a backward dive to the steps. The arrow flew over him, slicing the crown of his hat, then smashed into the stomach of a terra-cotta warrior on the other side of the corridor. The warrior, who was holding a battle-ax overhead, toppled.

Indy rolled away as the heavy ax cut a groove in the step where his neck had been. The warrior disintegrated into a jumble of shattered clay and human bones.

Indy sat up, brushed the brown dust from his clothes, and shook his head. "I'm getting too old for this—"

The step beneath him dropped down a few inches, followed by the hiss of air being forced through bamboo tubes.

"—stuff."

A stone marble popped from the mouth of one of the warriors and bounced down three steps before Indy caught it. The marble was green, streaked with white, and Indy rolled it between his thumb and forefinger. It was substantial and smooth, the kind he would have called a shooter when he was a kid.

"This is supposed to be scary?" Indy asked as he tossed the marble in the air and caught it palm-down. "Better try harder, Qin."

Another marble bounced past him, this time a red one.

Then he heard the sound of a hundred marbles hitting the floor above him, and rushing down the corridor. Indy stood and took a few more steps down the tunnel, and each step sank a little more. Soon a hailstorm of marbles were dribbling from the mouths of each of the soldiers, and the sound of the stone marbles pouring down the stairs grew thunderous.

A river of red, blue, and green overtook him.

Indy stood for a moment while the marbles swept past, then the surge become irresistible. It knocked Indy's feet out from under him and swept him along with the spherical tide, which crashed into walls and knocked over terra-cotta warriors as if they were bowling pins. Swords and knives fell from long-dead hands, and crossbow bolts whizzed in every direction. More marbles were added to the mix as they spilled from the broken clay figures.

The noise was painful.

The carpet of marbles made the tunnel as slippery as ice. Indy tried to slow his descent by grabbing hold of the soldiers, but clay arms and legs broke off in his hands. He winced as a fallen sword sliced through his leather jacket and nicked the flesh of his right shoulder.

"Okay, *this* is scary," Indy said.

He pulled his hat down over his ears with both hands and tucked his legs into his chest as the tide carried him swiftly down the spiraling passage.

The corridor opened onto a funnel-like pit, where thousands of marbles swirled around the rim like water about to disappear down a drain. The weapons and the pieces of clay and bone, which did not roll, slid directly into the depths of the pit.

Indy took the bullwhip from his belt and, as he swirled around the rim, lashed out blindly for the edge. Above, the whip found something to bite into, and Indy was soon dangling along the far side of the pit while the deluge of marbles washed over him.

Indy peered into the darkness.

"Whatever is down there," Indy said, "it can't be good."

He twisted for a moment before he managed to get a decent grip, then he began to haul himself, hand over hand, up the length of the twelve-foot whip. When he looked overhead, the beam of his electric lamp was reflected by a dozen glittering points of light. At first he thought he was looking up at the night sky, because the points seemed to make up familiar constellations—but the lights faded when he turned his head.

The slope of the pit began to lessen, and Indy soon had his legs beneath him as he scaled the last few feet. When he reached the top, he stood.

He felt as if he had come up through a drain in the bottom of the world. The end of the whip had caught the wing of a stone dragon that straddled the funnel on its hind legs and tail and that held the moon in its jaws. Indy knelt down, unsnared the whip, and became entranced as his lamp revealed the seas and craters etched on the ivory moon. It was about the size of a cantaloupe. The harsh electric light bounced from its ivory surface and bathed the chamber in soft, artificial moonlight. Suddenly aware that thousands of things sparkled in his peripheral vision, Indy turned his head.

Indy found himself in the middle of a jeweled sea, traversed by miniature sailing ships of silver and gold. Above, a canopy of diamonds shone in a midnight sky. The ceiling looked like an inverted bowl studded with jewels, and he could just touch the highest point with his fingertips. The floor of the chamber was flat and appeared to be about fifty feet in diameter. Continents were represented by patches of brown and green, but they were not arranged in the familiar pattern that Indy had become accustomed to since grade school. Instead, they were all ajumble, with Africa, India, and Asia encompassed by a single sea. The Americas and the poles were

missing, and the world apparently ended just beyond southern Europe. The continents were studded
with landmarks in precious metals.

Indy was off the coast of a storybook China,
where a Great (but miniature) Wall serpentined
around foothills of jade. The Yangtze and its tribu-
taries were flowing mercury. The center of the universe, Peking, was marked by a glittering temple.

Indy was stunned. During a more rational moment, his senses might have reeled at the sheer vol-
ume of treasure in the room, in terms of monetary
and historical value. But Indy was enchanted,
caught in the spell of Qin's perfect world, half be-
lieving that he must be dreaming in his bed at the
little house in Princeton, New Jersey. Gulliver-like,
Indy stepped over the rim of the funnel and reached
down to touch the bejeweled world.

His weight activated some ancient leveling device. Behind him, the moon fell from the dragon's
jaws and began to swirl down the funnel. He dove
after it, managed to get his fingertips on it, but was
suddenly jerked back. The strap of his satchel had
caught on one of the claws of the dragon's feet, and
he hung upside down beneath the stone monster
while the moon circled the neck of the funnel, then
disappeared.

Indy closed his eyes and listened to the pale orb
rattle down a system of pipes below him. Then there

was a sharp mechanical sound, followed by the gurgle of water.

This might be bad, Indy said to himself as he tried to untangle the strap. He was unsure whether he would be safer remaining in the treasure room or risking escape through the series of traps that he knew must lie beneath him.

Already a fine mist was wetting his cheek. Indy sucked his lungs full of air and closed his mouth. In another moment the mist had become a trickle, and then a torrent. He grabbed his fedora just as it was swept from his head. Indy dangled from the strap like a leaf trapped in a storm drain. Even above the rush of the water he could hear a set of massive gears churning below him, and he imagined the brittle cracking of bones as they were crushed to splinters between stone teeth.

Indy could feel the strap weakening against the weight of the water, and although he tried to pull himself up to grasp the stone appendages of the dragon, he could not. When his lungs could stand it no longer he gasped for air, and was punished by a mixture that left him sputtering.

Then the water subsided.

He heard the ivory moon land back in the jaws above him. The sound of rushing air slowed and then stopped. Indy allowed himself to relax for a moment, hanging like a wet sponge. He was glad he had been unable to undo the strap from the dragon's claw.

"Finally." He sighed. "A break."

Then the strap, which had been tested nearly to failure by the action of the water and the abrasion of the stone, broke. The movement jostled the stone dragon, and the moon fell once again from its jaws into the funnel.

Indy slipped into darkness and disappeared down the shaft at the bottom of the funnel. The orb followed after. In a few yards the shaft curved, and from the fleeting illumination provided by the electric light Indy saw a tiny trapdoor that was the right size for the miniature moon to pass through. He turned, seized the ivory ball, and clutched it to him like a quarterback facing an overwhelming offense. He knew the trapdoor would trigger the deluge once again and that this time, caught in the confines of the shaft, he would drown.

He had almost stopped tumbling when the shaft curved downward again, and Indy found himself dumped on his hands and knees in a layer of mud and unidentifiable muck in a new chamber. This layer of soft but disgusting material lined the bottom and sides of a deep pit. Indy got to his knees and examined the palms of his hands. Mixed in with the slime were tiny shards of bone. He wiped his hands on his trousers, snatched the ivory moon up, and placed it in his satchel. He tied the broken strap of the satchel together and slipped it over his shoulder.

Then he examined the rest of the chamber.

On either side of him were massive stone cylinders, obviously meant to press together under the force of the water and crush the offender. Above the pit, on a jade throne positioned to oversee such gruesome justice, was Qin. The emperor wore an armored breastplate and ornate helmet. Bits of leatherlike flesh still clung to the skull, as well as some wisps of black hair. At his feet were a half dozen skeletal concubines.

The ceiling was domed, and in the center was an eight-sided aperture. There was a symbol on each side of the aperture, and Indy recognized them as the eight symbols used in the *I Ching,* the Book of Changes.

Indy climbed up over the killing wheels and into the chamber proper, where he paused before Qin and tipped his hat. "What an ego," Indy said. "You must have left yourself an escape route, just in case your corpse came back to life. After all, you were a god."

Indy searched carefully, then found what he was looking for. On the right side of the throne, within reach of Qin's dead fingers, were five bronze levers.

Indy kneeled, then carefully inspected them. Odds were that only one of them would reveal a passage out; the other four were sure to be deadly traps. Even if an intruder reached Qin's throne, there was still an 80 percent chance of not getting out alive.

Indy stood and gazed into Qin's vacant eye sockets.

"What were you thinking?" Indy asked.

Numbers three and five, which Qin and his contemporaries probably considered divine, were the best choices, Indy decided. But which to choose?

Indy looked at his watch. The crystal was broken and the hands were frozen just shy of four o'clock. Time was running out when the watch had stopped, and Indy wasn't sure of how long ago that had been.

Indy reached for lever five, then hesitated.

"You wouldn't have made it this easy," Indy said finally. "Maybe it doesn't matter if you choose three or five. Perhaps it's more a matter of where you're standing—or *sitting*."

There were five broad flagstones surrounding the throne—two in front, two on the sides, and one in back.

"Move over, Qin."

Indy climbed up onto the jade throne and sat as gently as he could in the emperor's lap. Still, a cloud of dust rose from the corpse. Indy winced. Then he reached down, grasped lever number one firmly in his right hand, and tugged.

The flagstones in front of the throne fell open with an explosive sound that reminded Indy of a trap being sprung on a gallows. At the same time, the aperture in the center of the domed chamber opened. A rumbling shook the throne room as tons of fine sand poured from the aperture and into the shaft that had been revealed.

Then, as the sand stopped, the throne began to rise.

Above, Indy could see a glimmer of starlight in a pinkish sky. Below, he could see the shaft beneath the throne as it rose from the floor. Indy fought an urge to jump down. Whatever happened, the safest place in the entire tomb was probably sitting with Qin.

The throne was rising at an angle of several degrees off center, so that even though the sand fell into the shaft in front of it, the throne would rise up through the same aperture.

As it rose, it gained speed.

The throne passed through the aperture in the ceiling, twenty feet above the floor, and continued up at the same slanting angle. Indy could smell the fresh night air, and he could see a wider circle of fading stars at the end of the shaft.

The throne was going even faster now, and traversed the last hundred feet of shaft in a few seconds. Suddenly it was thrust from the side of the mountain and stopped, in a cloud of corpse dust, with a jerk. Qin's skull rolled from his shoulders, bounced once on the arm of the jade throne, then disappeared down the mountainside.

Indy was thrown from Qin's lap, but managed to grasp lever number five on his way over. It was the wrong one. He felt the mechanical click, then the throne began to recede back into the side of the mountain.

Below him, Indy heard a gasp.

"Ai!"

A squad of Japanese soldiers, who had been holding Lo at bayonet-point, were looking up in slack-jawed wonder at the spectacle of the jade throne, what was left of the emperor, and Indiana Jones hanging in the morning sky. Lo made use of the moment to flee, and none of the soldiers turned to chase him.

Given the choice between the certain death of being crushed against the side of the mountain and probable death at the hands of these Japanese raiders, Indy choose the latter. He released his grip on the lever and dropped to the feet of the Japanese soldiers.

The mountain rumbled, and the shaft seemed to disappear. Then, the round door where he had entered—which Lo had replaced before the soldiers arrived—gave a shudder and was sucked inward as the tomb regained its original pressure differential.

Indy greeted the soldiers with a wry smile and a salutation in Japanese:

"Ohio gozaimash'ta."

One of the soldiers made a move toward Indy with his bayonet, but the squad leader knocked it aside.

"Not to tell us good morning!" the squad leader screamed at Indy in English. "Not to say anything! What is your name?"

Indy was silent.

"What is your name?"

"You told me not to say anything."

"Silence!"

The squad leader drove the toe of his boot into Indy's ribs.

"You didn't have to do that," Indy said, doubling over in pain.

"What is your name?"

"Babe Ruth," Indy said.

"Stand up."

Indy stood.

The squad leader took the Webley from Indy's holster and stuck it into his own belt. Then he took the satchel and removed the ivory moon from it. He held it up for the others to see.

"Hey," Indy said. "This is still China, and that belongs to the Chinese."

"Property now of Imperial Japanese Army," the squad leader said. "You have strayed into Manchukuo, you stupid American. Now we take you into custody to help you get back safely."

2

MASTER SOKAI

The prison cell was dark, damp, lonely. Since his capture at Mount Hua, Indy had seen nothing but the back of an Imperial Army truck and the interior of the prison, which he had entered in the dead of night. They had taken everything from him, including his clothes and papers, and had given him nothing in return except a uniform that was little more than rags.

What light and fresh air that visited the cell came from a small barred window high above Indy's head. The prison had no electricity. When the sun went down and the light from the window died, the cell was plunged into darkness until the next morning. The cell was cold at night, and when it rained the water splattered down from the open window and dampened the pile of straw that served as a bed.

The latrine was a bowl that was emptied once a day.

Indy had no idea of his location, or what the Japanese intended to do with him. He saw no other prisoners. The guards brought a bowl of cold rice and a metal can of fetid water twice a day, and Indy was thankful they had thought to feed him at all. He suspected they were keeping him alive to learn more about the interior of the treasure tomb; otherwise, they would have killed him on the spot.

On the fifth day of his imprisonment, a pair of soldiers dragged him out of the cell. The soldiers differed from the slovenly, dim-witted provincial guards that brought the cold bowl of rice every day; these were well-groomed and sharp-eyed career soldiers. The younger was clean-shaven and had exceptionally fine features and jet-black hair, and even so it took Indy a moment to recognize that this soldier was a woman. She wore a heavy canvas flight suit over a tan service uniform, and at her collar Indy spied the yellow-and-red ribbon of a second lieutenant. The other soldier was heavier, a few years older, and powerfully built. He was bald, his jaw was heavy, and his eyes seemed to be furrowed in a perpetual scowl. He wore the dark brown coveralls of a warrant officer, and over his left arm was a white armband emblazoned with the rising sun. Both wore peaked caps with a gold star on the crown.

As these new soldiers dragged him down the corridor, the regular guards stepped oafishly out of their way and saluted, but refused to make eye contact with them.

That's a bad sign, Indy thought.

They threw Indy into a room that was bare except for a pair of straight-backed chairs and a wooden bench. There were no windows, and light was provided by a kerosene lamp that hung from the ceiling. The lamp's wick needed trimming badly, and the flame was ragged and belched carbon up the smoky globe and onto the ceiling.

The soldiers placed Indy roughly in one of the chairs, then stood at attention behind him.

On the bench were Indy's clothes, his satchel, his papers, the whip, holster, and revolver, even the ivory moon. The clothes had been cleaned and pressed.

Standing on the other side of the room was a man in a knee-length black trench coat. He was young—perhaps twenty-five—of average height, slightly built, with brown eyes and shortly cropped black hair. His cheeks were smudged, and even from across the room Indy could smell the odor of petrol and exhaust fumes. Around his neck hung a pair of aviator goggles, and beneath them were a white silk scarf. He was smoking a cigarette with such practiced nonchalance that he reminded Indy of a leading man in a Hollywood film.

He motioned for the soldiers to leave. They bowed and backed out of the room.

"Are you well?"

The man spoke English with no trace of an accent.

"Well enough," Indy said.

"Good."

The man reached into the pocket of his trench coat and casually drew out a pack of Lucky Strikes. He offered the pack to Indy.

"I don't smoke," Indy said.

"I did not think you did, Dr. Jones," the man said as he returned the cigarettes to his pocket. "I did not find any evidence of it in your things. But then, smoking is somewhat customary in prison. One of the few freedoms inmates enjoy."

With the cigarette dangling from his mouth, the man stepped up on the chair and adjusted the flame of the kerosene lamp. It burned more brightly now, with less smoke.

Indy blinked at the sudden brilliance. He ran a hand over his jaws, feeling a forest of stubble that was fast becoming a beard.

"Get to the point," Indy said.

The man smiled.

"Forgive me," he said. "This is somewhat awkward, isn't it? I must apologize for your treatment. I hope the squad that brought you in didn't hurt you too badly. No? Good. My name is Master Mishima Sokai. I work for the foreign office in Tokyo."

"So you're a spy," Indy said.

"Yes, and a rather good one," Sokai said with a smile.

"Then you can tell me why your goons dragged me here," Indy said. "I'm a professor of archaeology at Princeton University and was conducting legitimate research on Mount Hua when—"

Sokai held up his hand.

"Do not raise your voice, please," he asked pleasantly. "I am not easily intimidated, and I know more about you than even your colleagues on campus do. This secret life you lead is quite fascinating. Wherever Dr. Jones goes, trouble seems to follow. That cannot be a coincidence."

"Let's just say I have a talent for it."

"Indeed," Sokai said. "And I can appreciate your need for discretion."

"Since you seem to know so much about me," Indy said, "why don't you tell me something about yourself." Without asking, he reached out and pulled his clothes from the table. Sokai cocked an eyebrow, but did not stop him from changing.

"In addition to being regarded as Nippon's top spymaster by those in a position to know, I am also a fighter pilot, a *chutai* leader with the 24th Sentai of the Imperial Army Air Force."

"And I thought the goggles were just for fun."

"Actually, being a pilot has its advantages. No train or boat schedules to deal with, superior firepower, and the advantage of firsthand aerial reconnaissance."

"Fascists seem to be particularly fond of aircraft, I've found," Indy said. "What are those two that left the room? Your gunner and bombardier?"

"No, they are the other pilots in my *chutai*," Sokai said. "Lieutenant Musashi and Warrant Officer Miyamoto. We fly Ki-10 Type 95 biplane fighters. The Type 95 flies at a ceiling of nearly 10,000 feet, has a top speed of 248 miles per hour, and is armed with a pair of 7.7-millimeter machine guns in the nose."

"Do you have a picture of it in your wallet?"

"I appreciate wit," Sokai said, "but only when used sparingly. Like a precocious child, you are beginning to try my patience. See that it doesn't break."

Sokai stared at Indy a moment to make his point, then continued: "Let's see, what are the usual questions I am asked? I speak English well because I was schooled in the West. My father was a foreigner, a *gaijin*, a diplomat. My mother? A geisha who had the misfortune to fall in love with him. I was born the day in 1904 he was executed as a spy during the Russo-Japanese War. So you see, I have grown up *gaijin* in my own land. I have become quite a fan of American films, American cigarettes, and American clothes."

"But your politics are decidedly Imperial."

"America is just a hobby," Sokai said. "But Japan is the land of my ancestors. Besides, we're on the same side. We aren't at war."

"Tell that to the Chinese," Indy said.

Sokai laughed as he dropped the butt of his cigarette on the floor and ground it out with the heel of a well-polished shoe.

"Life is a struggle," he said. "I am a student of *Bushido,* the way of the warrior." Sokai reached inside his trench coat and withdrew a samurai sword. He held it front of him, upright, in a two-handed grip.

"Often, the old ways are the best," he said. "This blade is more than five hundred years old, and still it is the sharpest edge known to man."

Indy began to speak, but Sokai held a finger to his lips.

"The swordsmith who made it devoted ten years of his life to the process. It was forged only after the workshop had been purified and offerings made to the deity that would inhabit the blade, which was made of a single lump of iron ore. The blade was heated, hammered, and folded five thousand times, and each time it was cooled in the snows of Fuji to temper it."

"I've heard the stories," Indy said as he bent over to tie the laces of his boots.

"The spirit that enters the blade is a reflection of the piety of the maker," Sokai continued. "Sometimes, when the swordmaker's mental state was marred by a bad thought, an evil spirit would enter the blade. But it would not be known until the blade had drawn its first blood."

"I've got the feeling you've already found out."

"That was known long ago," Sokai said. Then he nicked the ball of his thumb with the blade, drawing a sliver of blood. "One should never sheathe an edged weapon without its having tasted blood. Otherwise, the hunger can grow overpowering."

In one graceful, practiced motion Sokai drew the back edge of the sword along the fleshy V between his left forefinger and thumb to guide the blade into the scabbard, then slipped the weapon home.

Indy looked at Sokai without comment.

"I always keep this blade on my person," Sokai said. "One never knows when the need for it will arise."

"I prefer more modern methods," Indy said. Then he reached for the Webley.

"Go ahead," Sokai said. "It's empty, of course."

Indy broke open the cylinder. Sokai was right.

Then he closed the gun, returned its familiar weight to the holster.

"And what of this?" Sokai said as he plucked the whip from the bench. "Surely you don't consider this modern? Slaves have been feeling the lash of the whip since time began. What an odd choice."

Sokai tossed the whip.

Indy caught it.

"Sometimes," Indy said, "the slaves turn the whip against the masters."

"An idealist," Sokai said. "How charming."

"What do you want?" Indy asked as he donned his hat.

Sokai picked up the ivory moon.

"From the tomb of Qin."

"If you say so," Indy said.

"Don't you wonder how Qin's astronomers knew the moon was round? And with such detail that they etched the craters and mares on the far side? We still don't know what *that* looks like. She never turns her back to us."

"Get on with it."

"I'm after not only treasure, Dr. Jones," Sokai said as he placed the moon in Indy's satchel. "I'm after power. Ancient knowledge. Magic. It is a force which all cultures before us understood. The ancient samurai, for instance, studied more than just the art of war. They also cultivated their talent for painting, music, literature, the play of positive and negative forces in the universe, and the use of incantations and spells. The soldiers told me quite a tale about your emergence from the mountain. Something about the ghost of the emperor dropping you at their feet?"

"They must have been drunk," Indy said as he slipped on his jacket. "I was so excited after I found this thing that I tripped going back down the mountain to tell my guide about it. That's all."

Then he picked up his hat, brushed some dust from the crown, and placed it in the satchel. He slung the satchel over his shoulder.

"Preparing to leave?" Sokai asked.

"Wouldn't you?"

Sokai reached down, picked up a wooden crate the size of a hatbox, and placed it on the bench. The crate was painted black, and the top was hinged and padlocked. Sokai produced a key from his pocket, unlocked the top, and swung it open.

He pushed the box across to Indy.

"Ever seen one of these?"

Inside was a helmet-shaped device, made of very old-looking iron.

"It's called the nutcracker," Sokai said. "Yes, that's right. It's used for cracking tough nuts." He tapped his own skull.

"It's lovely," Indy said.

"As I said, the old ways are often the best," Sokai said as he took the device out of the crate. It had thick screws protruding from the areas that would fit over the eyes, ears, and mouth. The halves were closed by a pin that slipped into the clasp from above. Sokai removed the pin and swung the halves open to reveal corkscrew spikes inside. They were black and crusted with dried blood.

"And you intend to use that on me?"

"If I must," Sokai said. "But I hope it won't come to that."

"Don't hold your breath."

"Very funny," Sokai said. "And very brave, in the face of being made progressively deaf, dumb, and blind. Ah, I see that I have your attention now. That is how it works—first one ear goes, and then the other. Then the tongue is ruined. Finally, because most of us prize our sight above all, first one eye is taken, and then comes the great darkness. But don't despair. Most nuts crack before it comes to that."

Sokai looked sympathetically at Indy.

"Or, you can avoid all of this unpleasantness and simply tell me the secrets of Qin's tomb," Sokai said. "I am particularly interested in getting in and out alive, as you apparently have."

"Go fish."

Sokai called to his aviators. When they came, he spoke softly to them in Japanese.

"*Hai,*" they each said and bowed curtly before beginning their work. They seized Indy's hands, wrenched them behind his back, and attempted to bring his wrists together so they could bind them with a cord.

"What's wrong?" Sokai demanded when they were unable to bring Indy's hands together.

"The *gaijin* is strong," Lieutenant Musashi complained.

"How strong could he be?" Sokai snorted. "He's twenty years older than you, and he's been on prison rations for nearly a week."

"Yes, Sokai Sensei," she said. "We will try harder."

In the struggle, the lieutenant's hat was knocked from her head, and a cascade of silky black hair fell from beneath it.

"Why do you look so surprised?" Sokai asked. "Did you not think the lieutenant's features were overly fine, that the voice was a little too feminine?"

"I knew she was a woman," Indy said. "But I didn't know she was this beautiful."

Then Sokai snapped his fingers.

Warrant Officer Miyamoto struck Indy on the back of the head with his fist, hard enough so that Indy saw stars. Pushing Indy into a chair, Miyamoto seized a wrist in each hand, grunted, and brought them together while the lieutenant bound them with cord.

"Good," Sokai said and drew close. "Hold his head."

He opened the nutcracker wide, screwed the spikes out, then clamped it over Indy's head while the others held him still. Indy fought until the helmet was closed. He could feel the tips of the spikes scraping against his eyelids, his ears, and his bottom lip when he moved even slightly. The only direction he could move his head, he soon found, was backward.

"There," Sokai said. "All set. Are you comfortable, Dr. Jones?"

"No," Indy mumbled.

"Of course you're not! Who would be?"

The soldiers stepped away while Sokai moved behind the chair and placed a hand on the screw handle that drove the spike over the right ear. Sokai slowly turned the handle.

"This is how it begins," Sokai said. "The anticipation of so much unnecessary pain. The sound of the screw turning, so close to your ear, followed by the feeling of the spike as it touches your outer ear— there, you jumped, you must have felt it—and then the awful agonizing seconds as it travels into the ear canal toward the tender membrane of the eardrum. And when the eardrum breaks, there is acute pain and a roaring sound—ironic, from an ear that has gone permanently deaf."

"You're enjoying this too much," Indy tried to say without stabbing his lip or driving the spike farther into his ear, but it came out unintelligible.

"Sorry," Sokai said. "You had your chance to—"

Indy kicked out, catching the edge of the bench with the toe of his right boot. The bench tipped over, and as it did, a corner crashed into the lamp, bursting the globe and extinguishing the flame while dousing the room with kerosene.

The room went dark.

Indy tipped backward, and as the chair went over with him the back of the helmet caught Sokai in the chest. It knocked the air out of his lungs, and Sokai fell to the floor, gasping.

Indy's right ear was ringing painfully and he could feel blood trickling down his neck, but he forced himself to keep moving. He untangled his arms from the chair back, got to his knees, and drove his chin to his chest while shaking his head. The pin slipped out of the clasp and the helmet fell to the floor with a bang.

The soldiers called for their master in the darkness.

Sokai was still struggling to draw a breath, but his hands were outstretched, searching.

Indy got to his feet. He backed against the wall,

so that he could search with his still-bound hands, and felt frantically for the door.

Sokai clutched Indy's leg in the darkness.

Indy tried to kick him away, but couldn't. Then, in the struggle, the cord binding his hands snapped, and he punched blindly toward where he thought Sokai's face would be. He was rewarded with the *smack* of knuckles meeting flesh.

Sokai, however, did not stop. He caught one of Indy's jabs in his hands, turned the wrist, expertly locked the elbow, and drove him to the floor. With his face jammed against the floor and Sokai on top of him, Indy could not reach far enough with his right hand to defend himself. Then his groping right hand found a piece of broken chair leg.

Indy swung the wood, haymaker style, and the extension was just enough to connect with his opponent's chin. Sokai's head snapped backward, he released his grip on Indy, and he swayed for a moment before he fell forward—into the open front half of the nutcracker lying on the floor.

Indy could not see what was happening, but he was shocked at the sound it made, a wet hollow sound like that made by driving an ice pick into a watermelon.

Lieutenant Musashi also knew the sound.

"I am blinded," Sokai said matter-of-factly, as if

it were someone else's eyeball that had been impaled on a rusty metal spike.

Musashi's alarm for her master turned instantly to a thirst for revenge.

"Stop!" she commanded, and the barrel of her semiautomatic pistol sought Indy in the darkness, wavering this way and that.

A second before the shot rang out, Indy instinctively felt that a gun was being aimed his way, and he flattened himself against the floor. The report was deafening in the small room, and the orange muzzle flash froze their positions as if a photograph were being taken—Sokai on the floor with the mask attached to his face like a living thing, Miyamoto in a fighting crouch but unsure of which way to go, and the lieutenant with a 1914 Mauser pistol held in front of her with both hands. The round pockmarked the wall behind Indy, then the room went briefly back to darkness.

Lieutenant Musashi squeezed off two more rounds, the sparks belching from the muzzle of her Mauser. The second shot missed, but her third found its mark. The slug hit Indy in the left shoulder, driving him through the wooden door and out into the corridor outside. A searing pain went from his collarbone down to the tips of his fingers.

Indy scrambled to his feet, shaking off pieces of the broken door, and stumbled down the hall. There was a barred window at the end of the corridor, and a trio of guards in front of it. The guards scattered when they saw Musashi step out of the doorway and level the automatic handgun their way.

She aimed carefully at the center of Indy's back and pulled the trigger. The trigger, however, was stuck; the gun had misfired, with a casing jamming the chamber.

Indy put his right arm over his face and plunged into the window. The bars gave way in a shower of old mortar and broken glass.

Musashi cursed fluently in English and threw the worthless foreign gun down in disgust. She barked orders at the prison guards to form a squad and go after the American. Then she screamed for them to bring back the first doctor they could find and to send for the best doctor in the province.

They looked at her blankly.

She repeated the orders in Japanese, even more ferociously than before. Then she walked back into the room, where Miyamoto was cradling Sokai in his arms.

"Is he dead?" she asked.

Miyamoto shook his head.

"But he might as well be," he said.

3

THE ROPE TRICK

Indy fell into the muddy street outside the prison and attempted a forward roll, but his nonresponsive shoulder left him on his back. His shoulder was throbbing and numb at the same time, the way your thumb is when you hit it with a hammer while trying to drive a nail. He didn't think the bullet had struck bone, but it was difficult to be sure. He grimaced and tucked his left arm protectively into his jacket, leaving the sleeve empty.

Then he was on his feet and running.

It was dusk and he made for the shadows that pooled beneath the gables of a deserted warehouse at the end of the street. Apart from a pair of chickens that scolded Indy for his rudeness, the street was deserted.

Posters in Chinese and French tacked to the weathered fence declared that the warehouse had been seized by the Imperial Army, was the property of the emperor, and trespassers would be shot. Indy had some difficulty scaling the fence, and as he dropped to the ground on the other side, he could hear the steady *tromp-tromp* of boots coming down the street.

The warehouse was a dark cave inside, and Indy could hear the cooing of pigeons in the rafters. He made his way quickly through the darkness, found a door at the rear of the building, shouldered his way past it, and discovered the end of a crooked, narrow alley.

The alley was a makeshift home to many dozens of families who had been displaced by the Japanese, and Indy had to hurdle cooking fires, squeeze between packing crates, and duck beneath clotheslines. Once he had to flatten himself against a doorway as a squad of soldiers passed at the intersection of a nearby street, and he held his finger to his lips to urge quiet from a family living in a crate as they stared impassively at him and ate from bowls of cold rice.

It was apparent that he was heading deeper into the older section of the city, but he had no idea which city. When he asked where he was, those brave enough to answer or to ask if he was hurt badly spoke a dialect he didn't understand. So he kept pressing on, hoping to find a landmark or some other sign that would give him a clue—and an idea of which way to run for safety. But every block looked the same as the last, other than its being more crowded and difficult to traverse.

Exhausted, Indy finally slowed to a walk.

A Japanese soldier on a motorcycle pulled up to the intersection of the last street Indy had crossed. He let the bike idle while he swung the handlebars to the left and right, searching the intersection with the beam of the headlight. The beam revealed the blood that Indy had trailed. The soldier shouted in Japanese and honked furiously to attract the attention of the other soldiers, then gunned the bike's engine and tore down the alley while refugees scrambled to get out of the way.

Indy heard the shouts and began to run.

The motorcycle soldier continued at breakneck speed down the alley, cutting through clotheslines and scattering cooking fires. He finally hit a clothesline that refused to yield, and that promptly snatched him from the seat of the bike.

Indy emerged from the alley into a public square in the city's old quarter. A thousand or more people were standing shoulder to shoulder to see a performance taking place in the center of the square on a traveling stage made from an old flatbed wagon.

The stage was lit by hanging lanterns and candle-powered footlights.

A blonde woman in dark robes covered with the usual assortment of hex symbols delivered a magician's patter in English, assisted by a dark-haired girl of perhaps sixteen. The teenaged assistant wore a yellow, loose-fitting silk outfit, including a tasseled cap with bells.

The magician paused every few sentences to allow a Chinese translator to give a more or less accurate account in the local dialect.

Indy shouldered his way into the crowd.

The magician pointed to the right. There was a bang, followed by a red scarf that floated out of a puff of smoke. Indy ducked involuntarily at the report. The magician pointed to the left. Another bang, and a green scarf floated down.

"Have you liked our show so far?" the magician asked.

The translator asked the crowd.

There was scattered applause and the beating of walking sticks on the ground.

"Well, the best is yet to come!" she promised. "Please show your appreciation by whatever you can spare—a bit of change, some food, a good wish if necessary. While my assistant, Mystery, passes the basket for donations, let me tell you something about our family."

She paused to allow the translator to catch up.

Indy noticed that more Japanese soldiers were beginning to arrive around the square. He worked his way deeper into the crowd, toward the stage.

"My name is Faye Maskelyne, and we are members of the world's first family of magic. Those of you who have visited fair London certainly know of our reputation, and those of you who have not had the pleasure will tonight see some of our finest illusions. But why, you might ask, are a mistress of magic and her able assistant touring for pennies in far-off venues when they could be earning a fortune and adulation undying from the comfort of their ancestral home?"

The translator had a bit of trouble with this last.

"I'll tell you," Faye continued. "The answer lies in the photograph that Mystery carries with her basket. Take a good look at it, friends, and tell her if you've seen this man. He is the object of our search. His name is Kaspar Maskelyne, and he is Mystery's father. He is also, of course, my husband."

The Japanese had now surrounded the square. Lieutenant Musashi scrambled onto the hood of a truck for a better view. Her hair was still unbound, and she was directing the search with Sokai's unsheathed sword.

"Kaspar Maskelyne came to the mysterious East four years ago, searching for a book of secret knowledge told of by the ancient Arab scholar, Ibn Battuta." Faye snapped her fingers and a book danced high over the heads of the crowd. "This book—the legendary Omega Book—contains a complete record of the lives of every soul who will ever live on this earth, and all of the secrets of nature. Every religion refers to it. There are different names for it, but it is the same book. And it can only be found with the aid of the Staff of Aaron."

Faye snapped her fingers again, and the book disappeared. At the same time, a staff appeared from a cloud of smoke on the stage. Slithering around the staff was a snake.

"The same staff that Moses turned into a serpent before the pharaoh's magicians, that brought down the plagues upon Egypt, and that parted the Red Sea. The original magician's wand!"

Faye clapped her hands. The snake disappeared and a flowering almond tree took its place. The translator was having a difficult time keeping up, and the crowd seemed lost.

"You all know about Moses, right?" Faye asked. "The staff turning into an almond tree in the desert? Okay, let's move on. You've all heard of the rope trick, right? Announce the rope trick, for God's sake."

The translator did so, and the crowd made appreciative sounds.

Mystery placed the offerings basket and photograph at the feet of the translator and returned to the stage.

"Our old friend Ibn Battuta called himself the traveler," Faye said. "And for good reason, because in 1355 he went so far as to visit the court of the Great Khan, and it is there that Battuta first recorded an account of what has become the most famous conjuration in magic—the Rope Trick."

Mystery dragged an oversized trunk onto the stage. She opened it, retrieved a small spear from it, and reached into the trunk for the end of a coiled rope. She tied the rope to the haft of the spear, then stood at the ready with it.

"Many have tried over the centuries to duplicate the miracle that occurred that night in Khan's court, but none have succeeded—until now. In our extensive traveling we have learned the necessary black art, and are pleased to present it to you now."

Mystery handed over the spear.

Faye turned and threw the spear upward. It disappeared into the darkness. The rope followed behind, uncoiling from the box, then hung, clearly suspended in midair.

The crowd gasped.

The soldiers elbowed their way through the crowd in a slow and deliberate search pattern that would soon pin Indy against the stage. Faye noted the uniforms moving through the audience, but pressed on with her act.

"There is an ogre living in the clouds," Faye announced. "He guards an immense treasure. He has vowed to rip anyone to shreds who attempts to steal it. But you, my lithe assistant, are up to the challenge."

Mystery's head swiveled from side to side.

"Up!" she commanded and pointed at the rope.

Mystery was having none of it.

Faye shook her head and looked at the audience. She again pointed at the rope and commanded Mystery to climb it.

The assistant backed away.

Faye produced a wand from her robes and aimed it at the assistant. She mumbled some words that sounded like pig Latin, and the assistant pretended to be irresistibly drawn toward the rope. She stepped into the box, then grasped the rope with both hands. Slowly, she began to climb the rope hand-over-hand, and the sight of her ascending the rope was made even more dramatic because she did not use her legs to propel herself upward.

"That's one athletic assistant," Indy mumbled as he turned up his collar and slouched against one of the wagon wheels. Two of the soldiers were now almost close enough to touch him.

Faye aimed her wand again.

In a puff of smoke, the assistant disappeared into the darkness. At the same instant, Indy ducked beneath the wagon and, in a running crouch, made for the other side. When he emerged, another soldier was waiting for him.

Indy ducked back beneath the wagon.

Above, Faye was calling elaborately to her assistant, and Mystery was answering in a far-off voice. Then there was the sound of a terrible fight, screaming and the ripping of cloth, and a few bits of tattered yellow silk floated down. Many of the pieces had conspicuously large drops of "blood" on them, and Faye picked one of these up and regarded it sadly. Then she drew her wand and began to recite a string of mumbo jumbo that grew in intensity as she made lazy circles with the wand.

It was dark beneath the wagon. Indy was crouching, waiting to see what the soldiers would do, when someone butted against him.

They both recoiled in surprise.

"Who are you?" a female voice asked.

"Who are *you*?" Indy asked.

"I'm the assistant," Mystery said as she crawled past. "You're not supposed to be under here. Go away."

"I'm hiding from those goons out there," Indy said.

"Saw 'em," Mystery said as she moved to a trap-door that was hanging open. It was beneath the oversized box that the rope had come from. "Sorry, mister, but I've got a show to finish."

The mumbo jumbo above them stopped.

"That's my cue," she said as she climbed into place. "Good luck."

There was an explosion, the usual smoke, and Mystery jumped from the box, restored.

"Good luck," Indy snorted as the soldiers began crawling beneath the wagon.

The Maskelynes were a hit in Manchuria. The crowd yelled, clapped, and stamped its collective feet. Faye clasped Mystery's hand and together they took a long, dramatic bow.

Then, the crowd began to ooh and aah again as Indy climbed out of the magic box, followed by the heads of a pair of bewildered-looking soldiers.

"Sorry," Indy said over his shoulder as he slammed down the lid and sat on the box.

"Don't mention it," Faye said over the audience's laughter. "They seem to like broad comedy. And you seem to be bleeding. Are you hurt badly?"

"I'll live," Indy said as he fought to keep the lid down. Then, he added: "I hope."

"Silence!" Lieutenant Musashi screamed from the hood of the truck. "Stop the American. He is a criminal. You there, on the stage."

"Us?" Faye asked.

"Stop him!"

"What do you want us to do?"

"Grab him, hold him."

"We can't do that," Faye said. "He's not part of the act."

"Then you will be in prison with him," Musashi said as she scrambled down from the truck. The crowd parted for her and the upraised sword.

Indy was fighting a losing battle with the box lid, as five soldiers were now pushing upward against it.

"The rope," Mystery said beneath her breath. "It's attached to a wire which is hung from the roofs of the buildings on either side."

"I don't think I can climb," Indy said.

"You'd better try," Faye said with a smile as she took another bow. "Mystery, why don't you help him."

Mystery smiled at the crowd as she walked slowly over to Indy, stepped up on the box lid with him, then reached down and set the lock. "There's a trick to it," she explained. "There's a counterweight on the other end. When I trip the cable, you're going to fly up like a bird." She took the end of the dangling rope and hitched it beneath Indy's shoulders.

"What about the two of you?"

"Don't worry about us," Mystery said.

"I'll stay here and fight," Indy said. "Let me—"

"How much do you weigh?"

"A hundred and seventy," he said.

"Too bad," she said.

"Why?" Indy asked. "Is that bad?"

"The rope is rated for a hundred and fifty," Mystery said and stood on the lever, behind the box, to trip the cable. Indy rose gracefully into the air, beyond the reach of the lantern light.

"Shoot him!" Lieutenant Musashi screamed.

The confused soldiers pointed their guns into the darkness, but did not fire. No target was visible, and they could not overcome their reluctance to fire indiscriminately in a populated area.

"What are you waiting for?" Musashi asked as she jumped up on the stage. "Fill the air with bullets."

"But Lieutenant," a sergeant stammered. "We have no lights. The square is filled with people. All of the surrounding buildings are occupied as well."

"You have hesitated too long," Musashi said through clenched teeth. "The American has had time to escape. Gather your men and search the rooftops. And, Sergeant—report to me later for disciplinary action."

"Yes, Lieutenant."

"You there, and you," Musashi called to a pair of the nearest soldiers. "Arrest this woman and her trained monkey. Cut some of that rope and bind their wrists. They will be taken to the provincial prison and charged with helping an Imperial enemy escape."

Mystery held her hands out in front of her, but the soldiers wrenched them behind her and tied them together with a three-foot section of rope.

Mystery giggled.

"That's too loose," she said. "It's going to fall off by itself. You had better make the knots tighter."

The translator, who was still at attention at one side of the stage, translated.

The soldiers showed their disbelief, but remade the knots. Both made ugly faces as they tightened them, and while they congratulated themselves on their strength, Faye slipped her hands inside her voluminous pockets and palmed a pair of smoke bombs in each hand.

The soldiers started toward Faye, but Mystery whistled before they reached her.

"Hey, guys," she said, holding the limp rope in her right hand. "Want to do this again? You just can't do it right. I told you it was about to come undone."

The soldiers grunted and turned angrily back toward Mystery. They didn't need the translator to interpret the mocking tone of her remarks.

Faye threw the smoke bombs.

The stage was enveloped in smoke.

When it cleared, Faye and Mystery were gone. So were the basket of money, the photograph, and most of their props. The only thing they left behind was the oversized magic trunk—and the pair of Japanese soldiers, whose hands were tied together.

Musashi batted smoke from her face. Then she stared at the trunk, held a finger to her lips, and tiptoed over to it. With a two-handed grip on Sokai's sword, she drove the blade down through the lid. When she withdrew it, the blade was smeared with red.

"Ah!" she said.

She ran a thumb along the blade, then tasted the red stuff.

It was sweet and tangy.

She threw open the trunk. It was empty. The sword had pierced a rubber bladder filled with catsup, kept in a pocket in the lid of the trunk, that the Maskelynes used in their human pincushion act.

Musashi cursed in three languages.

While Musashi and the soldiers continued to search the square and the surrounding rooftops, the Maskelynes were boarding a freighter a half-mile away. Indy sagged between them as they struggled up the gangplank.

"What city is this?" Indy asked.

"Luchow," Faye said.

"Port city," Indy said. "Formerly a French colony."

"At least he knows his geography," Mystery said.

"Say good-bye to Luchow, mister," Faye said as they reached the deck of the freighter.

"Where are we going?" Indy asked.

"You should care?" Faye asked.

"Right," Indy mumbled. "Anywhere is better than here."

"He's lost a lot of blood," Faye said to Mystery. "We've got to find him some help."

The captain of the *Divine Wind* was resting his elbows on the rail, smoking a Russian cigarette. He had watched the trio struggle up the gangplank.

"Trouble?" he asked calmly.

"What does it look like to you, Snark?" Faye asked.

"I hope it doesn't follow you here," Snark said.

"You said if we ever needed a favor, we could count on you," Faye said. "Well, we need one tonight. Where is that old drunk you call a ship's doctor?"

"Below," Snark said.

"Pour some coffee down him," Faye said. "We need him."

"If you wish," Snark said. He flicked the cigarette

into the water. Then he smiled. "Oh, by the way. No smoking on board this trip."

"I wasn't planning on it," Faye said.

"You know this guy?" Indy asked sluggishly.

"Unfortunately," Faye said. "It's a long story, but Snark won me in a card game at Taipei. Mystery was dealing, and she was supposed to give the winning hand to me. But she had a little counting problem that night."

"*Mother*," Mystery pleaded.

"Snark's a gangster, but it worked out all right," Faye said. "We spent two weeks teaching Snark every card trick in the book, and he spent two weeks telling us which officials to bribe in what towns to search for Kaspar."

"Army trouble?" Snark asked.

"This man escaped from the prison."

"He's a sailor now," Snark said. "Australian, by the name of Smith. Hurt in a bar fight at the Orchid."

"What time do you cast off?" Faye asked.

"With the tide," he said, then looked at his watch. "A couple of hours."

"Can we go now?"

"No," he said. "We've already filed our papers with the harbormaster. It would attract too much attention. Besides, we need high tide to clear those rocks out there. We're riding too low in the water."

"Okay," Faye said.

"Welcome aboard," Snark said. "Take the American to the infirmary and I'll have sawbones meet you there. I'll also have the crew get your old cabin ready."

"Right," Faye said.

Indy woke to the smell of antiseptic and gin. The doctor, an alarmingly thin New Zealander with a pint of Gordon's gin stuck into the pocket of his dingy white coat, had finished stitching the wound closed.

"Ah, you're awake," the doctor said when he noticed Indy's eyelids fluttering. "Sorry, but we've got no proper anesthetic. Had to get that bleeding stopped. The slug passed clean through, but it made a nasty hole where it came out the front, beneath your collarbone. You're lucky to be alive, mate."

Indy moaned.

"Oh, I bet it hurts."

"The woman," Indy muttered. "The girl."

"They're safe on board," the doctor said. He tied off the knot, then admired his handiwork and took a slug of gin. "Or, as safe as they can be with Captain Snark in command."

"Are we at sea?"

"We're still in port," the doctor said.

"Where are we bound?" Indy asked.

"Don't you know?" the doctor asked and smiled, revealing a mouthful of neglected teeth. "Japan."

"No—"

The doctor pulled Indy up, then began to wrap a bandage around his chest and shoulder.

"We've got to get off this boat," Indy said.

"Brother," the doctor said, "you and me both."

Indy grimaced.

"I've got to go," Indy said. "The magician and her daughter are safe. I've got other places to go. But I'm so . . . tired."

"It's the loss of blood, mate."

"Maybe I'll just rest here for a few minutes," Indy said. "You know, gather my strength. Wake me in time to jump ship."

There was a knock on the door of the infirmary.

"Come in," the doctor said. Then, to Indy: "Relax."

Faye and Mystery walked in. Faye was dressed in a black robe tied with a red sash, while Mystery wore the dark blue uniform and cap of a Japanese merchant sailor.

"How is he?" Mystery asked.

"Not bad," the doctor said, "for a sixty-year-old man."

"I turn thirty-five this year," Indy said.

"That's different," the doctor said. "He'll live,

but you've got to consider the material I had to work with. This guy's got more holes in him than a screen door."

"Thank you, Albert Schweitzer."

"Who?"

"Never mind," Indy said.

The doctor shrugged as he picked up his tools.

"This boat's headed to Japan," Indy said. "I'm leaving, just as soon as I catch my wind. You've got to get off, too."

"We will," Faye said. "At the first opportunity. But we must stay put for now. It will be high tide in an hour, and that's when we're scheduled to sail."

"That's my cue to go," Indy said and struggled up. Then he paused. "What are you dressed up for, a Halloween party?"

"The clothes?" Faye asked. "We thought we'd better change. The only women normally found on freighters like these have been kidnapped into prostitution. Thousands have been taken from across Asia, of all nationalities."

"What's your story?" Indy asked Mystery.

"I always dress as a boy," she said.

"It's safer that way," Faye explained. "At least while she still has the build to get away with it."

Indy nodded.

"Come on," Faye said and helped Indy off the table. "You don't want to go back ashore at

Luchow. Let's get you to a bunk, so you can rest. I'll wake you if anything happens."

Indy had just closed his eyes when the door to the cabin burst open, followed by a bayonet with a rifle and a Japanese soldier on the other end.

The soldier spoke loudly and rapidly in Japanese and made rapid, jerking motions with the bayonet. Indy didn't know what he was saying, but it was obvious that he wanted Indy off the bunk.

Indy swung his feet over the edge of the bunk, but his head was spinning so badly that he followed them right to the deck. The doctor appeared in the doorway, slipped past the soldier, and helped Indy back onto the bunk.

"Glug, glug," the doctor said and mimed tipping a bottle.

The soldier laughed.

A sergeant appeared behind the soldier, and he was not amused.

He asked the doctor what was wrong with the American. The doctor told him in Japanese tortured by a New Zealand accent that the sailor was Australian, had gotten blind drunk that night, and had foolishly wound up on the wrong side of a knife fight with a three-hundred-pound Malay.

The sergeant spat.

"All *gaijin* look alike to me," he said as he hitched up his trousers. "Their feet are too big, their voices too loud, and they all smell like rotten hamburger. We have orders to search all of the ships leaving harbor tonight for a big, ugly American with a gunshot wound and a female magician and her apelike assistant."

"Knife, not gunshot," the doctor said. "Besides, his name is Smith and I was at the Orchid when the fight started. If I had not been, he wouldn't have been around to cuss me in the morning."

The sergeant reached beneath Indy's unbuttoned shirt and was about to lift the dressing when another soldier carried Faye down the corridor and into the room. Captain Snark was on their heels.

"Bring her back," Snark ordered.

"No," Faye shrieked. "Get me off this boat. This pirate has kidnapped me and intends to sell me into prosti—"

The sergeant backhanded Faye, hard enough that it split her lower lip. For a moment, she swayed, the silk gown began to slip from her shoulders, and Indy thought she would pass out. Then she gathered herself, wiped the blood from her mouth, and gave the sergeant a cold smile.

"I was hoping you were here to rescue me," she said.

"Shut up, please," he said in thick English. "You make good comfort woman. No take you away."

"*Domo arrigato,*" Snark said, and allowed the sergeant a slight, nearly imperceptible bow.

The sergeant grabbed Indy's jaw in his beefy hand and turned his chin to the left, and then to the right, while he inspected the cuts and bruises. Indy refused to focus on his piglike eyes, but he was not spared the sergeant's stinking breath.

"This is not the *gaijin* we are looking for," the sergeant said in Japanese. "This one stinks of gin and is obviously too stupid to have escaped the provincial jail."

Then he shoved Indy back down on the bunk, turned toward the door, and with a wave of his hand ordered the soldiers after him. Suddenly he stopped, grasped Faye by the waist, and pulled her roughly toward him. He give her an exaggerated kiss on the lips, then released her and slapped her bottom.

Indy was off the bunk and halfway across the cabin when the doctor grabbed him. "This fight is not worth dying for, mate," the doctor whispered as their footsteps echoed down the hall. "Let them leave. When that bloke is dying in some trench at the hands of a bloodthirsty Chinese warlord, or blind from syphilis at having taken comfort once too often at a well poisoned by his comrades, we'll be having a drink to his stinking memory at the

International Hotel in Tokyo. Do you know the place?"

"I know it," Indy said.

"Across the street is the white-walled castle of the emperor," the doctor said. "Ducks and geese swimming peacefully in the moat. Every once in a blue moon you can get a glimpse of the Hirohito himself, a small man in a great hat and tails who, I think, would rather be a gardener. Not too ambitious for a living god, eh?"

Indy looked at the doctor in admiration of his ability to soothe with his voice and his appreciation for the beautiful amid the chaotic.

"Surprised? I wasn't always a wreck with ruined teeth and cyanotic hide," he continued as he turned to Faye and inspected her bleeding lip. "I've had a succession of careers—journalist, lawyer, doctor. Well, not really a doctor, but I will pass for one in these latitudes. I used to sit at the bar at the International Hotel, drinking saki from those little ceramic cups, congratulating myself on my civility and watching the world slip away. A little like the emperor."

"How so?"

"Japan is such a damned fine island, and look at the wretched hands it is in now. But we did it to ourselves, didn't we? You know, the Japanese even gave up the gun once, after the Portuguese brought it four hundred years ago. But Nippon has managed to become just as modern and bloodthirsty as the rest of us. The world is at war again, but most folks don't know it yet—it began here, two years ago, and nobody cares. Well, mate, they will."

He produced some swabs and antiseptic from his medical bag.

"This is going to hurt, but I wouldn't want to chance where that brute's knuckles have been today," he said as he dabbed at Faye's lip.

"What happened to you?" Indy asked.

"I woke up," he said. "And I couldn't stand it. I know what is coming, because I learned this business of patching people up as a corpsman during the Great War. So I became a drunk, and now I pass my time pretending to practice medicine on a rusting hulk captained by a Japanese smuggler. Tending war orphans in Manchuria while Snark is out gathering whatever illicit cargo he can find."

"Pretending?" Indy asked and felt his wound. "Now you tell me."

"Well, most of it came back to me," he admitted as he finished ministering to Faye's bottom lip, now stained with iodine.

"What's your name?" Indy asked.

"Bryce." When he spoke the name, he seemed to

grow a little taller. "Montgomery Bryce, Oxford, class of 1923."

"Jones," Indy said and held out his hand.

They shook.

"Yes, I know," Bryce said. "I've seen your mug in the newspapers. But a gentleman doesn't comment until the introductions have been made."

Then there was a jolt, and Bryce smiled as he steadied himself against a bulkhead. "Ah, we've cast our moorings. The tugs are taking us out into the harbor. Soon we'll be rid of this stinking piece of real estate."

"What is Snark carrying this trip?"

"He doesn't confide in me," Bryce said.

He knelt on the floor, closed up his bag, then looked at Indy and gave him a glance that was filled with an unspeakable mixture of horror and guilt.

"You know, Jones, it's quite true what I said," he said. "But it's not the whole cloth. While pretending not to see the rape of Manchuria, I fell in love with the concubine of a petty warlord collaborating with the Imperial Army. The girl's name was Si Huang, she was seventeen, and she was the most gentle creature I have ever known. But honor bound her to her station in life; she would not flee to safety with me. The warlord, of course, found out. Do you know what he did?"

Indy closed his eyes.

"He killed her. Then he cut out her heart, cooked it up, and had it mixed into the curried pork I ate for my dinner that night."

The doctor gave a smile that projected no mirth.

"I have never eaten a bit of meat since," he said as he snapped his bag closed. "And just before I nod off to sleep at night—that is, if I'm sober—I will get a little whiff of curry, and the night terrors close behind."

The *Kamikaze Maru*—the *Divine Wind*—had been at sea for nearly ten hours when the pair of Kawasaki Ki-10 biplanes appeared on the horizon over her wake. Indy had heard the drone of the big radial engines, and he knew they could mean nothing but trouble.

He had slept in his clothes, so to finish dressing meant grabbing his hat and jacket on the way out of the cabin. It was dawn now, and the eastern sky was bronzed by the rising sun.

As Indy reached the bridge, the biplanes buzzed the ship.

Snark was on the deck, watching through a pair of binoculars as the planes flared and prepared for another pass. Faye, Mystery, and Bryce were already there.

Even without the binoculars, on the wings of

both planes Indy could clearly see the *hinamaru*—the rising red sun of the Japanese empire.

"Dr. Jones," Snark said. "You seem to be more trouble than you're worth. Somebody must have figured out which ship was unlucky enough to have you. Is there anyone back home who would pay good money to have you back safe and sound?"

"Not unless my old friend Marcus Brody can figure a way to make a museum piece out of me," Indy said.

"Too bad," Snark said. "These biplanes, they are too far out to sea now to turn back to Manchuria. They cannot land on the water, and they have barely enough fuel to reach the Japanese coast. Instead of a fuel pod, each carries a torpedo slung beneath her belly."

Snark handed the binoculars to Indy.

"Can you hail them?" Faye asked. "Negotiate, perhaps?"

"There's no radio on the *Divine Wind*," Snark said.

"I thought that after 1912—," Faye began.

"That's your world," Snark said impatiently. "The *Titanic* did not make a great deal of difference to us. In our world, shipwrecks are fate. For communication, we use signal guns, or flags, or rescue flares, instead of wireless. Unfortunately, that does not allow for two-way communication in this circumstance."

"I think they're about ready to send us a message," Indy said as through the binoculars he watched the biplanes line up on the stern of the *Divine Wind* for their attack. At seventy-five yards, the torpedo fell from the belly of the forward plane.

The mechanical shark left a stream of bubbles as it raced through the green water toward them. Snark turned the ship hard to port, then bellowed orders down the voice tube to evacuate the engine room and close the aft compartments.

"They're trying to sink us," Faye blurted.

"No," Snark said. "But they might manage to. They want to cripple us, to damage the old girl's rudder and screws and prevent us from escaping. If they had wanted to sink us, they would have hit us amidships with both torpedoes. But they don't know what we're carrying in the aft hold.

"*Brace for impact,*" Snark commanded.

Then he closed his eyes.

The torpedo struck slightly off-center, with a dampened *whomp!* that washed the stern with foam and sent a sickening shudder down the ship's keel.

Snark opened his left eye.

"Well, that wasn't so bad," Faye said after a moment.

"It's not over," Snark said as he tried the wheel. It

was locked hard to port. "We have revolutions on one screw, but all we can do now is sail in a circle."

"What exactly *are* we carrying?" Indy asked.

"Chinese fireworks," Snark said.

"Fireworks?" Indy shot back. "And you call yourself a smuggler?"

"They're illegal," Snark said defensively. "And you know you could lose a finger with some of those things."

Black smoke belched from the stern.

The first mate spun the crank on an ancient mechanical siren to sound fire stations, and the half dozen crewmen who were still below emerged on deck. One of them was struggling with a Browning Automatic Rifle.

"Give me that," Snark said, taking the BAR away. "Do you want to start a war with the entire Imperial Army?"

A grease-stained mechanic burst onto the bridge.

"Anybody hurt?" Snark asked.

"No, Captain," he answered in Japanese.

"Then get down there and douse that fire," he barked.

"We can't, sir," the mechanic said. "The engine room is flooding, and the fuel oil is burning on top of the water."

"Is the aft hold secure?"

"Yes, sir," the mechanic said. "I think."

The shriek of a skyrocket and the machine-gun rattle of firecrackers ended his indecision.

"No, sir, apparently not."

"Damn," Snark said.

The Ki-10 that had released the torpedo had swung around to inspect the damage and was now flying low and slow over the *Divine Wind*—which was, at that moment, exactly the wrong place in the sky to be. A crate of fireworks exploded, engulfing the stern in a fiery blossom of red and green and peppering the wings of the Ki-10 with hundreds of flaming, buckshot-sized pellets. The bottom wing smoldered angrily for a few moments, then burst into flame.

"He's going to have to ditch," Indy said.

Snark cursed elaborately in Japanese.

"We've shot down one of the emperor's planes," he muttered to Indy in English. "With smuggled Chinese fireworks, while harboring a trio of Western fugitives."

"Congratulations," Indy said. "You're moving up in the world."

The pilot of the Ki-10 deftly guided the crippled plane toward the sea. It touched the surface two hundred yards off the starboard bow of the sinking cargo ship, tipping up on its nose in a great spray of water, then settling heavily back down.

Snark calmly gave the first mate the order to abandon ship.

"How much time do we have?" Indy asked.

"Twenty minutes," Snark said. "Half an hour, at most. The water won't douse the fireworks—they are chemically fueled, and they will burn a hole through the bottom of our hull. Then, we'll have flooded four compartments, which is one too many for us to stay afloat."

"How about going after that pilot?" Indy asked.

"He'll drown soon enough," Snark said, then smiled. "Funny, but this old girl had the last laugh, didn't she?"

"No, I mean to rescue."

"Not a bad idea," Snark said. He nodded toward the biplane still in the air. "Make a show of it, maybe save my neck if I ever get back home to Nagasaki. Mr. Bryce, take one of the boats and fish the emperor's chosen out of the sea."

"I'll go with you," Indy said.

"Be quick about it," Snark said. "It looks like the crew have claimed the other two boats. The rest of you, go as well. As captain, it's fitting that I am last off."

"Faye, get your things," Indy said.

Faye nodded. Mystery started to follow her to the cabin, but Faye pushed her back. "Help them launch the boat," she said.

"Just get the picture," Mystery said. "And my bag of tricks."

"Don't let Snark fool you," Bryce told Indy as they released the lifeboat from its blocks. "There isn't a bit of honor about him—he just wants to make sure he cleans out the safe in his cabin before the first mate beats him to it."

"Does he have that much to lose?" Mystery asked.

"It's not much," Bryce said. "At least not by our standards. A few hundred bucks, the price of a new car in the States. But with the ship gone, it's all he's got."

They threw a net over the side and, when Faye returned to the rail, they clambered down it into the sixteen-foot boat. Indy was gasping from the pain in his shoulder by the time they had the oars in the water.

"Let me," Mystery said and took Indy's place at the oar. "Go to the bow; search for the pilot."

"We're lucky," Bryce said. "The sea is calm this morning."

Then they all flinched as another round of pyrotechnics erupted from the hold and shrieked up into the early morning sky.

"Luck," Indy said, "is a relative term."

They rowed toward the oil slick that marked the spot where the plane had gone down. The pilot was resolutely treading water, keeping her mouth just above water.

Indy laughed when he saw the silky mass of dark hair floating around her head.

"Lieutenant Musashi," Indy said. "Why am I not surprised?"

Musashi barked a scathing response in Japanese, then took in water. She coughed and spat, and her head bobbed under once before she could continue. She was obviously tired, near exhaustion, but she managed to add in English: "You are under arrest, Jones."

Mystery recognized the demeanor.

"This is the madwoman who was chasing you at the square?"

"Afraid so," Indy said.

Bryce left his seat to help Indy haul her in.

"Come on," he said as he extended the oar toward her. "Be a good little Imperialist and climb on board."

Above, the lone biplane was circling.

"Go to hell," Musashi said, then swallowed more water.

"Don't be difficult," Indy chided. "You're going to drown yourself if you're not careful. You know, we have every right to leave you out here."

Musashi shook her head.

"All right," Bryce said. "We're all under bloody

arrest. Now, get in the boat and make sure your bloodthirsty buddy up there sees it."

Musashi went under again, but grasped the blade of the oar with a trailing hand. Bryce hauled her to the boat, and Indy reached down with his good arm, grasped the fur-lined collar of her flight jacket, and lifted her over the gunwale.

"She weighs a ton in this thing," Indy groaned.

Bryce waved the oar in the air.

The biplane waggled its wings in response and departed toward the southeast.

Then Bryce threw down the oar and jammed his finger into Musashi's mouth to make sure she hadn't swallowed her tongue.

"Is she breathing?" Indy asked.

"I think so," Bryce said as he tipped her head over the rail and slapped her back. Seawater sputtered from her nose and mouth. When Bryce turned her back, she tried to fight him off, but had no strength.

"Help me check her for weapons," Indy said.

"Are you kidding?" Bryce asked. "She's just a kid."

"This 'kid' is the one who put the hole in my shoulder and sank our boat," Indy said. He unzipped her flight jacket, then stopped. "Uh, Mystery. Would you mind?" he asked.

"Love to," Mystery said as she came forward and

began to probe unknown pockets. "We've got a can opener, a compass, and some pocket change." She handed the things to Indy and dove into another pocket.

"Pay dirt," she said as she withdrew a .25-caliber automatic.

Bryce took the gun and slipped it into his pocket.

"Keep searching," Indy said.

"Papers," she said. "Looks like a passport and some other official-looking documents. Oh, look at the red ribbon. Isn't that cute?"

"Keep going."

"Okay," Mystery replied and felt down Musashi's pants legs to the tops of her boots. "Oh, you were right. What a wicked-looking little knife."

Indy inspected the switchblade, then threw it overboard.

When they returned to fetch Snark, the rest of the crew had gone and the hulk was dipping alarmingly toward the stern. He was standing casually, smoking a cigarette, a canvas bag slung over his shoulder.

He threw the bag into the boat.

"What took you so long?" he asked as he stepped down from his patch of deck into the lifeboat.

"It was complicated," Indy said.

"When the *Wind* goes under, the pull is likely to take us down with her," Snark said as he took the tiller. "We'd better put some water between us."

Although the *Kamikaze Maru* sank into the Sea of Japan, the water failed to extinguish the fire that had eaten through her belly. It continued to smolder even after the ship was on the bottom, marking her grave with a witch's cauldron of smoke and bubbles.

4

TY FUNG

The craft, small and large, that came to the aid of the refugees appeared seemingly from nowhere, summoned by the unwritten law of the sea and the fireworks over the grave of the *Divine Wind*. The crew accepted passage on a whaling vessel back to Japan, while Snark boarded a steam packet bound for the mainland.

"Good-bye, Faye!" Snark called theatrically as the packet chugged away, waving his hat and leaning dangerously far over the rail. "Until destiny brings us together again!"

"He certainly seems devoted," Indy said as he grasped hold of a rope net the crew of a junk had lowered over the side.

"Oh, he's just full of it," Faye said dismissively, although she blushed a bit.

Mystery was first up the net and onto the deck of the junk, then she extended a hand and helped pull Bryce over the rail. Indy was halfway up when Faye called to him.

"What do we do about her?"

Musashi was still in the lifeboat, looking sullen, her hands tied in front of her.

"Leave her," Indy said.

"We can't," Faye protested.

"Yes we can," called Mystery. "She tried to kill us, Mother. Listen to Dr. Jones. He's right."

"Being practical isn't the same as being right, Mysti," Faye said tiredly. "She's a human being. We can't leave her in the bottom of a lifeboat."

"Who's going to babysit her?" Indy asked.

"Not me," Mystery said.

Although Musashi was trying to control herself, her wide eyes betrayed her fear.

"I'm not leaving without her," Faye said.

"Then we'll give her a choice," Indy shot back. "She can come with us and behave herself, or we will drop her into the sea at the first sign of trouble."

"Do you understand?" Faye asked.

"Yes," Musashi said.

"Dr. Jones is quite serious," Faye said.

"I understand," Musashi said quietly. "But all of you are still under arrest."

"See what I mean, Mother?" Mystery asked. "She's impossible!"

"Then we'll just have to treat her like cargo," Bryce said as he tossed a rope down to the lifeboat. "Make her fast and we'll winch her up."

Faye hitched the rope beneath Musashi's arms, and Bryce hauled her aboard the junk. She was still struggling as her feet touched the deck.

"This is going to be nothing but trouble," Indy predicted as Faye climbed up onto the deck.

The captain of the junk, a leathery old man who smoked a long-stemmed clay pipe, had been watching the display from the quarterdeck. He laughed aloud at Musashi's antics.

"I'm glad somebody's amused," Indy said.

"He seems to think that she's your girlfriend, old boy," Bryce said as he cast the lifeboat adrift. "He also thinks you have your hands full. And I must say, I quite agree."

"The Imperial Army won't be satisfied with an empty lifeboat," Indy said, attempting to ignore Bryce's enjoyment of the situation. "When they find it, I'd like them to think we drowned."

Indy pulled the Webley from its holster, leaned over the rail, and put five rounds into the lifeboat as it drifted past. The boat sank slowly to its gunwales as it swirled in the wake behind them.

"That will not fool Sokai Sensei," Musashi said.

"No," Indy said as he reloaded the Webley, "but it might just buy us some time. Mr. Bryce, let's have a chat with the captain, shall we?"

After a long and somewhat heated discussion, a deal was finally struck.

"The old Malay pirate who is running this junk wanted a hundred dollars American to run us to port," Indy reported as he rejoined the Maskelynes on the forward deck. "I gave him everything I had, which was thirty-five dollars and some change."

"Was it enough?"

"It'll have to be," Indy said.

"Where exactly are we headed?"

"Shanghai," Indy said. "Which is good, because I have friends there. We should arrive sometime tomorrow night. Until then, we just need to take it easy and lie low."

Faye nodded.

"And we can get you passage back to England."

"I beg your pardon?" Faye asked.

"We're American, Dr. Jones," Mystery said. "Mom uses the English accent onstage because people expect it, because Daddy is English. But Mother was born in Oklahoma."

"Okay," Indy said. "We'll get you back to the States, then."

"We're not going back," Faye said. "We're going to stay here until we find Mystery's father."

"But you have no business in this part of the world," Indy said. "It's dangerous, if you haven't noticed. You and your escape artist of an assistant are going to get yourselves killed."

"We were doing quite well," Faye said, "until you happened to crash the show. It wasn't the Imperial Army searching for *us*. And, if I recall, we were the ones who saved your hide, not the other way around."

"I was doing all right," Indy said.

Faye laughed.

"You were not," she said. "You were three steps away from being back in prison. And now that we're on the subject, what were you locked up for, anyway? You never told us."

"It's a long story," Indy said.

"I'll bet," Faye said. "And that alias of yours. Couldn't you think of something better than Jones? It shows a distinct lack of imagination."

"It's my name," Indy protested.

"But only on the days it isn't Smith, eh?"

"Mother," Mystery pleaded. "Please don't fight."

"He started it," Faye said. "I just want him to know that we're going to continue our search for

Kaspar, and that we expect him to repay us for the losses we've suffered because of him."

"You mean all of that was true?" Indy asked.

"Of course it's true," Faye said. "Do you think we would make all of that up?"

"It was such a good story," Indy said, "I figured it was just part of the act. Forgive me, but in my experience stage magicians haven't exactly been the most reliable of sources. But if what you say is true . . . *that* could lead to some interesting possibilities. I might even be inclined to stick around."

"How's your shoulder, Dr. Jones?" Mystery asked.

She was doing her best to change the subject.

"It hurts," Indy said as he stretched out on a mound of burlap and pulled the brim of his hat down over his eyes. He was silent for a moment, then asked: "Do you mean to say that your Kaspar really *was* searching for the Staff of Aaron?"

But before Faye could answer him, Indy was snoring.

As the junk continued her leisurely, dreamlike journey to the southwest, Indy allowed himself to sleep in order to cope with the pain from his aching shoulder. Driven by the wind and attended only by the sound of the water and the sails, the junk made for a timeless scene that could have taken place during any of a thousand previous Septembers. Shrouded in mystery and tradition, the castlelike junk made her way down the channel that separated Japan from occupied Korea.

By that afternoon the junk was crossing the East China Sea, bound for Shanghai. Although high storm clouds were building in the east, the day was balmy, the sea was calm, and the wind was moderate. The air had taken on that particular luminous quality that Indy had only seen in the East; the day seemed to shimmer in green and gold.

Then, early in the evening, a shadow crossed the sea.

The eastern storm clouds had been pushing a cold front before them, and it had finally overtaken the junk. The sunlight turned dull and the temperature dropped fifteen degrees in as many minutes, chilling the passengers and causing Indy to rouse from his sleep when he heard the words whispered on the lips of the crew: *ty fung*.

"Where are we?" Indy asked, coming to the rail.

"About a hundred miles off the Chinese coast, near Shanghai," Faye said. The wind was beginning to pick up, although it was not yet raining, and it blew her robes out behind her like a pennant. She was holding on to the rigging, looking over the choppy water to the battlement of dark clouds approaching from the east. Lightning bursts of pink and blue played at the base of the wall cloud, while beneath it poured the telltale streaks of wind and rain.

"What's that word they keep repeating?" Faye asked.

"*Ty fung,*" Indy said.

"What's it mean?"

"It's not good," Indy said.

"I'm afraid not," Bryce agreed as he struck a match, cupped his hands around it, and lit a cigarette. "It means typhoon. And considering how much the barometer has dropped in the last hour, and the time of year, I'd say they are bloody well right."

"A hurricane?" Mystery asked.

"They're called typhoons in these parts," Bryce said. "Willie-willies in Australia, *el baguio* in the Philippines, hurricanes in the Atlantic. But they're all basically tropical cyclones."

"Terrific," Mystery said.

"Too bad we don't have a radio," Bryce said. "I wonder what my old friend Clement Wragge will name this one. Clever, that Wragge. He's an Aussie weatherman who has taken to naming storms after women he admires or politicians he dislikes."

"Whoever heard of naming a storm after a woman?" Faye asked.

"Seems perfectly logical to me," Indy muttered.

"Can we outrun it?" Mystery asked.

"The storm is probably four hundred miles wide," Bryce said. "And they generally blow to the southwest, until they hit the coast. We're running dead ahead of it, and we don't have a prayer of making the mainland before it hits."

Musashi, who was sitting cross-legged on the deck with her hands tied in front of her, began to laugh.

"What's so funny?" Indy demanded.

"Even the weather is against you," she said.

"She really has a sick sense of humor," Mystery said.

"What can we do?" Faye asked.

"Nothing, I'm afraid," Bryce said. "Wait and watch, and hope we can make it to an island cove or some other shelter before the storm overtakes us."

Then Bryce took the pint of gin from his jacket pocket, drained it, and threw the empty bottle into the sea.

Sokai wore a black robe. His feet were tucked beneath him, with the big toes crossed, and his hands rested palm-down on his thighs. He lowered his bandaged forehead until it touched the hardwood floor, then held the position for a respectful three seconds.

When he returned to *sezen*, the sitting form, the candles on either side of the dark altar flickered. The flicker was reflected from the black-lacquered sheath of the samurai sword, which lay within hand's reach on the floor in front of him, and from the glass-framed likenesses of his dead masters that lined the walls of the dojo. The flicker was reflected also in the almond-colored iris of Sokai's right eye.

The other eye, still beneath seeping bandages, was useless now. The spikes of the nutcracker had also gouged out hunks of his left ear and cheek. Together with the clumsy stitches the village doctor at Luchow had used to close the wounds, the damage had turned Sokai's matinee idol good looks into something more Karloffian.

Sokai had been sitting motionless before the altar in the darkened training hall for hours, searching for the *boon ki*—the reason, the essence, the true meaning—of the thing that had happened. He had scanned the visages of the masters of Bushido that lined the walls, from his own Okinawan master all the way back to the fierce and gap-toothed countenance of Dharuma, the sixth-century founder of Zen Buddhism who also brought martial arts to the monks of the Songshan Shaolin Monastery. After reaching the monastery, Dharuma was said to have spent nine years in silent contemplation of a cave wall, listening to the sound of ants screaming.

One of the monks watching this feat of self-control was so moved that he cut off one of his own hands and offered it to Dharuma in sympathy.

The story, some felt, was meant to defy interpretation, another Zen koan that one is to reflect upon but never really to grasp. Intellectual understanding was an impossibility; the best to be hoped for was a sort of contemplative emotional acceptance.

But as Sokai allowed his fingertips to touch the bandages over his blinded eye, he believed he understood the message. The dark night of his life had been illuminated in the way that lightning reveals the secrets of a summer's night.

The sound of ants screaming had a name.

"Jones," Sokai growled.

And the name had become a curse.

The typhoon overtook the junk in a dark wall of wind and water that blotted out the sky. The hull of the junk was driven relentlessly forward on the storm surge, like a surfboard riding the crest of a wave. The captain and the crew had vanished at the first sign of the approaching storm, escaping in the small boats that trailed the junk like pilot fish on the belly of shark. They would weather the storm in whatever island shelter they could find; then, if the junk survived, they would return. If not, another ship always came along in time.

Indy and the others had fewer choices.

They had made themselves fast to a cargo hatch in the waist of the ship, with their backs against one another. Before the storm hit, Bryce had cut the rope binding Musashi's wrists. Indy had placed his fedora inside his jacket and zipped it up. Then he had intertwined hands with Faye on his left and Mystery on his right.

They could hear the storm approaching, and it sounded like a hundred steam locomotives rushing over the water toward them.

"Dr. Jones," Mystery shouted.

"What?"

"I'm scared."

"So am I," Indy replied. "But just hold on to my hand, no matter what."

The masts of the junk were carried away like twigs in the first great rush of water over the deck. The hull rolled completely over. For nearly a minute Indy and the others were beneath the water, holding their breath and holding tight, until the hull finally righted itself.

Pounded by ninety-foot waves and scourged by winds that sometimes reached two hundred miles an hour, the castle sections at the bow and stern were quickly broken away. The timbers of the hull poked up like skeletal ribs in the open places, and seawater foamed through in and out of the cargo hatch, but the waist section of the hull held together.

Then another wave tossed the hull in the opposite direction, and the hull rode the crest until it was suspended over a canyon of surging water.

Mystery screamed as the deck slid from beneath her feet.

Indy's hand tightened around her wrist.

She dangled for a moment over the abyss.

"Mysti!" Faye shouted.

"I've got her," Indy said.

At the same moment, Bryce's grip on the cargo hold failed and he plunged feetfirst into the angry sea, his white-jacketed arms windmilling all the way down.

Then Indy pulled Mystery to the protection of his side as the hulk came crashing back down toward the sea.

The storm continued for more than an hour unabated, but the relentless action of the wind and water rendered Indy and the others unconscious long before that. The cargo section of the hull was awash, but remained afloat. As the wind subsided, the hulk grounded itself at the shank of a hook-shaped islet.

Faye was the first to come around.

After making sure that Mystery was breathing normally, she untangled herself from the ropes that held her fast to the cargo door and arranged her clothes.

Then she shook Indy.

"Jones," she said. "Wake up."

"I'm awake," he insisted. "Where are we?"

"An island," she said. "It looks uninhabited. Probably uncharted. We've been blown pretty far off course, and I'd be willing to bet we're not in the neighborhood of Shanghai. But the storm's over."

"It couldn't be," Indy said, rubbing his eyes.

"It's so quiet," Faye said. "And look—up there. Clear sky."

"You're kidding."

"No," she said. "And birds flying."

"That storm had to be several hundred miles across," Indy protested. "It can't be over that quickly."

Faye struggled to her knees. She leaned over and patted Mystery on the cheek. The girl's eyes fluttered open, then stared up at her mother for a few long moments.

"Mr. Bryce," Mystery said. "I'm sorry he's gone."

"So am I," Faye said. "But it's almost like he gave

himself to the storm so that the rest of us could pass."

"I thought that, too," Mystery said.

"It was a tough break, that's all," Indy said in a hoarse voice as he unlashed himself from the cargo door. "But it's a miracle the three of us survived."

"Four," Musashi said through her exhaustion. "We are four in number. One Imperial officer and three prisoners."

"Sure," Indy said as he pulled his waterlogged hat from his jacket and put it on. "It's still a miracle, any way you want to slice it."

"That may just be the right word," Faye said. "Look."

A double rainbow stretched across the dome of sky behind them.

"It's not over," Indy said, suddenly comprehending. "It's just a reprieve. We're in the eye of the storm. Look down toward the horizon—you can see the wall clouds swirling all around us."

"What do we do now?" Faye asked.

Indy stood up.

Mystery winced sympathetically at the sound of his knees creaking and popping.

"We've got to find a place to ride out the rest of the storm," Indy said and rubbed his shoulder. "And we'd better do it in a hurry. If you look straight above, you can see that the center has already passed over us. The rear of the storm will be coming, and it will be just as fierce as what we've already been through."

"Look," Musashi said.

She was pointing up the beach.

The beach was littered with uprooted trees and other debris from the storm. But rising from a cluster of palm trees in the center of the island was a rough-hewn steeple, and on top of the steeple was a wooden cross.

5

LAZARUS ISLAND

The wooden cross was set upon a rocky promontory overlooking a lagoon. Beneath it, built from a cave in the volcanic hillside, was a fortresslike church with great copper-sheathed double doors.

Indy grasped the ring of one of the doors and pulled.

"It's locked," he said.

The wind was picking up, and it had begun to rain again.

"Is it occupied?" Faye asked.

"Somebody locked it from inside," Indy said.

The beach itself was ringed with a few huts, and several deserted outriggers had been pulled high up on the sand. A couple of well-weathered signs in French declared the island a restricted trade zone.

Indy beat on the tarnished copper with his fist, then picked up a chunk of volcanic rock and continued knocking. It began to rain harder. A bolt of lightning struck a palm tree fifty yards down the beach, and the concussion of the blast nearly knocked them down.

"Hey!" Mystery yelled with renewed vigor. "Inside the church! We need shelter!"

The door was suddenly unbolted and swung open by a robed and misshapen figure with a kerosene lantern.

The four scurried into the cavern.

"Thanks," Indy said as he shook water from his hat. "The storm just about got us—again."

"*No entrez,*" the man said.

"Mister, there's a hurricane out there," Mystery said. "Or hadn't you noticed?"

"I notice," the man said in a thick French accent. His voice was coarse, as if he had not spoken in a long time. "The island is restricted. You cannot stay."

"Sorry," Indy said. "But we really don't have a choice. The storm sank our ship."

"Restricted how?" Faye asked.

"Forbidden," the man croaked.

The man put the lantern on the floor. His face was hidden by a bulky hood, and he stepped sharply away when Indy tried to put a friendly hand on his shoulder.

"Sorry," Indy said. "Look, we'll be no trouble. Four half-drowned castaways seeking refuge from the storm. We'll be on our way as soon as possible. Do you have a radio so that we can send for help?"

"Stay here," the man said.

He left the lantern and walked back into the darkness.

"What was that all about?" Faye asked.

"I don't know," Indy said, "but he must have great night vision."

The storm raged outside and water seeped beneath the double doors and pooled on the flagstones. Indy picked up the lantern from the floor, held it high, and swung it in an arc around them. The flickering light revealed dusty pews jumbled haphazardly together.

"Looks like it's been some time since they've had services here," Indy said.

"It's been years," Faye said.

"I don't like it," Musashi said. She was clutching her arms in an attempt to keep from shivering. "This reminds me of the ghost stories my grandmother tells, where travelers are caught in a storm and seek the shelter of a strange castle. They never turn out well."

Finally, another lantern appeared at the far end of

the church and made its way toward them. It was held by a much taller robed man than the first.

"I apologize for Henri," the man said in a French accent. "We don't get many visitors. As a matter of fact, we get no visitors at all. I understand that your ship went down. Are there any other survivors?"

"No," Faye said. "We are all."

"I'm sorry," the man said. "Was it a commercial ship? What line?"

"No line," Indy said. "It was a junk. I'm not even sure what its home port was."

"Then there is no need to send a radio message, or to search for others," he said. "Come, please. We must get you warm and dried off."

The man led them down a flight of stairs into a bunkerlike area outfitted with a long wooden table, a few cots, and a bookcase. He held a candle to the chimney of the kerosene lantern until it ignited, then used the candle to light three others on the long wooden table.

"You will be more than safe here," he said.

"I can hardly hear the storm," Indy said.

"Yes, the order certainly built a fortress for themselves," the man said cheerfully as he fed kindling to the potbellied stove in the center of the room. "This room hasn't been used since the last of the brothers left. It is strange, but the old prohibitions about segregation still hold some sway."

"Pardon me," Indy said. "I don't mean to be rude, but could you tell us where we are?"

The man stopped his work with the stove, unaware that a blotchy forefinger remained in the burgeoning flames.

"Watch out," Indy said as he pulled the man's arm back.

"Damn," the man said as he dashed the fire out against his robes. "You really don't know? You didn't see the signs?"

"They said something about a trade zone," Faye said.

"Yes," the man said slowly as he closed the stove door and sat down on the nearest chair. "This is Lazarus Island. It was founded by the Order of St. Lazarus. It's a leper colony."

"Lepers," Musashi hissed.

"I'm told that I am not that hideous," the man said as he pulled back his hood to reveal a pale, middle-aged face that was normal, except for some pinkish-gray splotches alongside his nose. "My hands, however, are taking a beating. I have no feeling in my fingers, you know. Sorry for the stench of burning flesh."

"That's the restriction," Indy said. "Trade money."

"Yes, we are forced to use trade money," the man continued. "Fear of contagion, you know. At first it was the French, and then when the order fell apart some decades ago, the Americans issued the trade money and enforced the restriction. The church has not been in use since before the Great War."

"So this is a U.S. possession?" Indy asked.

"Nobody will claim Lazarus Island," the man said and laughed. "But they make us use the segregated money anyway, to buy those things we cannot make for ourselves."

"Is it contagious?" Mystery asked.

"I'm sorry," Faye said and clutched her daughter by the shoulders. "Please forgive our manners. Pardon me, but I don't know your name."

"Pascal."

"Monsieur Pascal."

"It is quite all right," he said. "It is contagious, mademoiselle, but it is not spread from such casual contact as exchanging money. Those who live among lepers know that most healthy people have a natural immunity. In fact, many people who are married to lepers never contract the disease. Ignorance, I'm afraid, has done far more damage than the disease itself."

"Is there a cure?" Mystery asked.

"No," Pascal said. "There is no cure."

"Not yet," Indy said. "But there will be."

"I wish I could believe it," Pascal said. "But, we

make do as we can. That is why Henri was so stand-offish with you. The penalties for breaking the trade restrictions can be quite severe. Society has not only made us outcasts, I'm afraid, but turned us into criminals as well."

"You're in good company," Indy said.

"How many of you are there?" Faye asked.

"Nearly one hundred," Pascal said. "Mostly men, but some women."

"And you are their representative?" Indy asked.

"Their spokesman, their doctor, their lawyer, and their priest," Pascal said. "Please accept our hospitality. When the storm abates, I will send food. Until then, I suggest you dry your clothes and get some rest. With the exception of one, you are Americans?"

"Yes," Indy said.

"Tomorrow morning, I will attempt to contact the USS *Augusta*. She is the flagship of the Asiatic fleet and has been cruising between here and Shanghai for weeks, in an attempt to show American strength. Perhaps, if she is not too far out, she can pick you up."

"You have a radio," Indy said.

"Of course," Pascal said.

"Nuts," Musashi said.

"Should I also attempt to contact the Imperial—"

"No," Indy said. "And please, don't let this

woman near that radio transmitter. Mystery, would you mind doing the honors?"

"Love to," Mystery said. "Got some rope?"

Pascal looked shocked.

"Is that necessary?" Pascal asked.

"Very," Indy said.

"May I at least get out of these clothes?" Musashi asked through chattering teeth. "I'm cold."

"There is another room," Pascal suggested. "A smaller one. It has a door which can be barred from the outside. Like this one, it is underground, and has no other exits. It has a stove as well."

"That will work," Indy said.

"I'll help her," Faye said as she took one of the blankets. "Come on, Mysti. Let's give Dr. Jones some privacy."

"I'd rather stay in here," Mystery said.

"Afraid not," Faye said.

"What about your shoulder?" Pascal asked Indy. "I noticed that you seem to be injured. Is it broken? Do you require medical care?"

"No," Indy said. "Thanks. It will heal, in time."

"As you wish," Pascal said. "Until morning."

Now alone, Indy removed his soaking clothes and hung them over the chairs to dry. Then he wrapped himself in a blanket and lay down on the cot.

He was tired, but he was not yet ready to sleep.

His eyes scanned the dusty volumes in the old bookcase.

Most of the titles were in French, catechisms and lives of the saints. There was a German dictionary with a badly torn cover. The two books in English were the memoirs of U. S. Grant and a copy of the King James Bible.

Indy reached for the Bible.

He blew the dust from its cover, then turned to Exodus.

In his dreams, Indy searched.

Perhaps it was the influence of revisiting the Old Testament before sleep, or the hundred anxious moments of the past few days, or the knowledge of being deep within the earth. For whatever reason, Indy found himself in a biblical landscape of pyramids and idols, sand and sun, searching endless corridors and impossibly serpentined passages for a glimpse of a shadow that remained always just around the next corner.

Often he was near enough to recognize the sound of her voice, sometimes he could catch a fleeting glimpse of her face, but never was he close enough to actually touch her. His frustration was compounded because a part of him knew it was just a dream, and that he could never catch up to her.

"Who's Alecia?" Faye asked when Indy woke.

"Pardon?"

"You were talking in your sleep," Faye said. She was sitting at the table, eating breakfast from a plate of fruit that Pascal had brought. "I don't mean to pry, but she seemed awfully important. Is she your wife?"

"I've never been married."

"Your girlfriend, then."

"No," Indy said.

He sat up and rubbed his eyes.

"What time is it?" he asked.

"Just after dawn," she said. "I went outside a little while ago. It's beautiful, now that the storm has passed."

"Where's the lieutenant?" he asked.

"Still asleep," Faye said. "So is Mystery."

"Why aren't you?" Indy asked.

"Never could sleep in," she said. "Are you going to tell me?"

"Tell you what?"

"About Alecia."

"Why should I?" Indy asked.

"Because we're friends," Faye said. "Because we have been through a life-and-death ordeal together. Because we're glad to be alive. Because I want to know, and because you want to tell me."

"I don't."

"Are you in love with her?"

"I was," Indy said.

"But not anymore."

"Look," Indy said. "I'll give you the short version, okay? I once knew a woman named Alecia. We made each other miserable. Then she died."

Faye was silent.

"Satisfied?" Indy asked.

"No," Faye said. "Can you talk about it without being angry?"

"You're making me angry."

"I don't think so," Faye said. "You're angry about this woman, and you have been angry for a long time. I just didn't know until now what you were angry about."

"Look, this has nothing to do with me anymore—"

"It has everything to do with you," Faye said. "Think about it. People just don't drop everything and take off for a foreign land unless they are unhappy or unfulfilled. I know—I speak from experience."

"Kaspar was unhappy?" Indy asked.

"He didn't ask me to follow," she said.

"Then why do you search?"

"Because I love him," she said. "Because Mystery needs her father—or, at the very least, needs to know what happened to her father. And because I'm sharp enough and strong enough to find him, and I could never forgive myself if I didn't try."

Indy coughed.

"This is making you uncomfortable," Faye said.

"It's not the sort of thing that fellows talk about with their friends," Indy admitted.

"We'll stop," Faye said.

"Good," Indy said.

Faye reached down and picked up the Bible.

"Saying your prayers?" she asked.

"Reading about the Staff of Aaron," Indy explained. "I understand why Kaspar was fascinated—it was the original magic wand. It could find water, bring plagues, smite your enemy. As long as Moses held it up, the Israelites could not lose in battle."

Faye smiled.

"When I was a child," Faye said, "I would close my eyes, open the Bible, and read a verse at random. It seems pretty silly now. But the verses always seemed to make sense."

"But no longer?"

"No," she said.

"What do you think has changed?"

"I have," Faye said. "I grew up."

"Children are given to magical thinking."

"You don't believe in magic, Dr. Jones?"

"It depends on your definition," Indy said. "If you mean the kind of entertainment that requires a willing suspension of disbelief from an audience that should know better, then the answer is yes, I enjoy it."

"No," she said. "I mean real magic."

"If science has taught us anything," Indy said, "it's that there's no such thing. Magic, superstition—these are things of the past."

"Science is just another belief system," Faye said. "It is a good system, but it is not the only system. Nor does it explain everything. Do you believe in God, Dr. Jones?"

"Yes," Indy said.

"Good," Faye said. "At least that's something. You suspend your belief in science to allow room for faith in something you cannot prove exists, but which you posit because of a conviction that goes beyond the rational. Would it be so hard to admit that magic may work as well?"

"If there were proof," Indy said.

Faye smiled.

"That's what Kaspar was looking for," she said. "Others might seek the Staff for the riches or the power it could bring, but Kaspar was after something else. He wanted an affirmation that magic worked, that miracles could still happen."

"The original magic wand," Indy said.

"Yes," Faye said.

"But it's hopelessly lost to antiquity," Indy said. "It may even be a myth."

"If it is," Faye said, "it is a particularly well-documented myth. The Old Testament mentions it often. In Exodus, it turns into a snake and gobbles up the serpents conjured by Pharaoh's magicians. It turns the Nile to blood and helps to call down the ten plagues upon Egypt."

"Frogs, gnats, and swarms of flies," Indy said. "Boils, fiery hail, and locusts. Cattle die. Darkness upon the land. Death for the firstborn of Egypt. But even if you found it," Indy asked, "how would you know it was *the* Staff? If it survived, it would be nothing but a dried-up old stick by now."

"You mean how could you tell it from a fake?" Faye asked. "The Bible describes it as a rod, made of almond, with Aaron's name on it. And then, of course, how many dried-up old sticks can perform miracles?"

"You can't be serious," Indy said.

Faye returned his unblinking stare.

"Well," Indy said, "if it works, then I guess it would settle the question of magic once and for all."

Faye smiled, and was about to add something when Mystery burst into the room.

"Dr. Jones!" she said. "Mother! Come quickly. There's an airplane in the lagoon."

*   *   *

Indy and Faye followed Mystery outside. The brilliance of the sunshine on the beach made Indy blink.

Sitting in the middle of the lagoon, like a lone duck on a farm pond, was a massive flying boat. It had four engines mounted on its single, overhead wing. The fuselage was shaped more like the hull of a boat than an aircraft, an effect that was reinforced by a series of portholes. On the nose, below the cockpit windows in black lettering, were the words *Pan American.*

From beneath the wing of the plane the crew was launching a small boat.

Pascal appeared at Indy's side.

"I did not expect you to be up so early, considering your ordeal yesterday," he said.

"When did the flying boat arrive?" Indy asked.

"A few minutes ago," Pascal said. "I made contact with the *Augusta* this morning," he explained. "They, in turn, contacted the flying boat."

"I didn't know Pan Am had passenger service in this part of the world yet," Indy said.

"They don't," Pascal said. "Their Clippers are limited to South America, I believe. But the radioman on the *Augusta* said they were testing a new aircraft."

As the boat neared the beach, Pascal became uncomfortable.

"If you don't mind," he said, "I have the morning's duties yet to perform."

"Thank you," Indy said.

"Thanks is not necessary."

"Oh, I think it is," Indy said and held out his hand. Pascal paused, then grasped Indy's hand in his.

"We won't forget your kindness," Indy said.

Pascal nodded, then disappeared into the cavern of the church.

The boat pulled up to the beach and the crewman rowing shipped the oars. A tall man in a blue jacket stepped from the bow into the surf.

"I understand you've had rather a tough go," he said.

"Just a small typhoon," Indy said.

"We were lucky enough to avoid it," the man said. "My name is Ed Musick. I fly for Pan American, as you can see, and we've been performing tests on the Sikorsky S-42. Beautiful, isn't she?"

"I'll say. I haven't seen one in years."

"Pardon?" Musick asked. "The S-42 just went into production."

"I mean, a flying boat," Indy said.

Musick smiled.

"We've also been exploring some airways and harbors for a possible China route next year," he said. "We received a radio message asking us to rescue some storm refugees."

"That would be us," Indy said. "Captain Musick, this is Faye Maskelyne and her daughter, Mystery."

"Ladies," Musick said and tipped his hat. "I'm afraid we can't return you to the States, since we're not equipped yet for passenger service. But our next stop is Calcutta, and from there you should have no problem getting passage back."

"That would be a great help," Indy said.

"Is your party ready?" Musick asked. "The radioman said there were four of you."

"We're almost ready," Indy said.

"What do we do with the lieutenant?" Faye asked.

"We can't leave her here," Indy said. "We'll take her to Calcutta and drop her off at the Japanese embassy."

"A Japanese national?" Musick asked.

"The only other survivor of our boat," Indy said.

"I'll go untie her," Faye said.

"She's tied up?" Musick asked.

"Wait," Indy said. "After you meet her, you'll understand."

As the flying boat ascended into the blue sky above Lazarus Island, Indy sank into the well-cushioned seat and pulled the brim of the fedora over his eyes. Faye and Mystery were gathered at the window, looking down at the azure lagoon, but Indy had been in so many airplanes that such sights had become routine. Instead, he was thinking about how he would phrase the telegram to Marcus Brody when they arrived in Calcutta, and where they would stay until the money arrived.

On the other side of the aisle, with her hands bound but her eyes bright and sharp, was Musashi.

She was planning as well.

6

JADOO

Indy pulled Musashi by the hand through the crowds that choked downtown Calcutta, with Faye and Mystery at their heels. Above the confusing mix of Bengali, Hindi, and Urdu—which everyone seemed to be speaking as loudly and as quickly as possible—there were the shrieking horns and growling engines of the incessant buses, the tread of tens of thousands of feet, and the universal cry of the curbside beggars.

"This is the noisiest city I've ever heard," Faye said.

"It's also the poorest," Indy said. "Thousands of these people sleep on the streets because they have nowhere else to go. Most of those fortunate enough to have a home live in the *bustees,* the slums, where there is no running water and no sewers. Starvation and disease are rampant."

"After the Depression hit, I thought Oklahoma was rough," Faye said. "But the more I see of the world, the more fortunate I feel to be an American."

"Don't forget that feeling," Indy shouted back.

After asking at every corner they came to, they eventually found the Japanese embassy, hidden from the teeming masses by an iron gate guarded by a pair of Imperial soldiers.

"Okay," Indy said as he untied the rope that bound Musashi's hand to his, "this is it. *Sayonara*."

She stood in front of the gate, rubbing her wrist.

"Hey!" Indy shouted as he waved his arms at the guards. "*Hai!* Come and get her. She's one of yours!"

"You should have killed me when you had the chance," Musashi said.

Indy leaned close to her.

"There's still time," he said.

The guards unlocked the gate and Musashi stepped inside. She immediately began barking orders in Japanese and pointing at Indy.

"They wouldn't dare—," Indy said.

"They would," Faye said as the soldiers came toward them.

"Run!" Indy said.

In a moment they were lost in the crowd. The soldiers stopped at the end of the block, unwilling to get out of sight of the embassy.

"Cowards," Musashi hissed when they returned.

After haggling with a pawnbroker for twenty minutes, Indy succeeded in pawning his wristwatch for ten dollars. Then, at the Western Union office next door to the pawnbroker, he sent a telegram to New York. Its briefness was dictated not only by the precarious state of their finances, but by Indy's reluctance to explain:

> TO: MARCUS BRODY, AMERICAN MUSEUM OF
> NATURAL HISTORY.
> FROM: INDIANA JONES
> IN CALCUTTA, NEED MONEY QUICK. STOP. NO
> QUESTIONS, WILL EXPLAIN LATER. STOP.

At Travelers Aid, they asked about the cheapest and safest place to spend the night. They were sent to the Atlas House, a somewhat run-down but still respectable hotel that catered mostly to middle-class English-speaking merchants. The Atlas charged two dollars per night, with board. They signed for two rooms.

As the desk clerk looked at their names, his eyebrows went up.

"Something wrong?" Indy asked.

"No," the clerk said. "It's just that Maskelyne is a name you don't see much. Had a Maskelyne stay here three or four years ago, as I recall."

"Kaspar Maskelyne?" Faye asked.

"I believe so," the clerk said.

"Are you sure?" Faye asked. "It's very important."

The clerk pulled an old register from beneath the counter and began to turn the pages.

"Yes, here it is," he said and turned the register around so that Faye could read the entry. "February 14, 1930. Valentine's Day. Staying in one of the same rooms you are."

Faye ran her finger over the signature.

"Which room?" she asked.

"Yours," the clerk said. "Two-oh-seven. Are you related to him?"

"I'm his wife," she said, choking back a tear. "This is his daughter."

"Who's that?" the clerk asked about Indy.

"A friend," Faye said. "Helping us look. My husband's disappeared."

"Why do you remember Kaspar?" Indy asked. "You must get several hundred guests each year."

"Well, we don't get too many that are magicians," the clerk said. "He would give little performances out here in the lobby area in the evenings, and talk to folks about magic and such. An awfully friendly fellow. He stayed here about a week."

"Do you recall anything else?" Faye asked.

"He asked me if I had ever heard of a bloke named Jadoo," he said. "Sure, I says, everyone has heard of the old Jadoo, the most famous magician in India. He asked if I could help him find an address on Bengali. It's at the edge of one of the *bustees*, and hard to find if you don't know what you're looking for."

"Do you have a pencil and a scrap of paper?" Faye asked.

"Certainly."

"Would you mind telling us how to get there?"

"Not at all," the clerk said. He wrote the directions down, then said, "That's an area you don't want to be caught in after dark. I'd wait until morning."

"We can't go now?" Mystery asked.

"He's right," Indy said. "Let's wait until morning."

"Mother," Mystery said. "This is the first good clue we've had."

"We've waited four years," Faye said. "Another night isn't going to make any difference. Besides, I'm tired and hungry, and we can't pay a visit on a fellow magician looking like shipwreck victims—which, of course, we are."

*   *   *

They found the shop on a narrow side street. They
had passed it twice before Mystery noticed the small
numbers on a faded red door that read 707. The door
opened on a flight of worn stairs that led to another,
more substantial door on the third floor. This door,
made of oak, had a carefully polished brass name-
plate attached—*Jadoo: World Famed Magician. By
Appointment Only.*

"How do you make an appointment?" Mystery
wondered.

"Let's find out," Indy said as he rapped sharply
on the door with his knuckles.

After a few moments a flap opened in the middle
of the door. A pair of bloodshot eyes peered out.

"We're here to see Jadoo," Indy said. "I'm
Indiana Jones, and these are—"

"So sorry," the squeaky colonial British voice
that went with the bloodshot eyes said. "By appointment only."

The flap slammed shut.

Indy knocked again, this time a little harder.

The flap opened.

"You don't understand," Indy said with forced
civility. "We need to see Jadoo the Magician on a
matter of some importance. We don't have time to
make an appointment."

"Appointment only," the voice snapped.

The flap closed again.

Indy rubbed his jaw, regarded the closed door, then pounded on it with the edge of his fist.

The flap did not open.

He pounded again, this time hard enough to bring plaster down from the aging ceiling.

"Stop," Faye said.

"I thought you wanted to see this joker," Indy said.

"I do," she said, "but not by tearing his building down."

"Be my guest," Indy said.

"Excuse me," Faye said and knocked lightly on the flap. "We're terribly sorry for the inconvenience, and I understand that all visitors should have an appointment. But if you would be so kind as to tell Jadoo that the Maskelynes are here to—"

The flap snapped open.

"What name did you say?"

"The Maskelynes," Faye repeated. "I am Faye Maskelyne, the wife of the great magician Kaspar Maskelyne, and this is our daughter, Mystery."

"Hello," Mystery said.

The flap snapped shut, and then there were the rattle of chains and the clicks of turning locks. The door opened, and a thin Indian man in a white jacket urged them in with a wave of his hand.

"I am the master's servant," the man said. "Call me Pasha."

"Thank you," Faye said.

They found themselves in an extravagantly appointed entrance room full of memorabilia of several decades of magic. The shelves were filled with books on magic in several languages and brimmed with props and other devices. The servant closed and locked the door behind them once they were in.

"I am sorry," he said, "but the master is out at the moment. He will be back very soon, however, and I am certain that he would like to see you. Do you care to wait?"

"We will wait," Faye said.

"Very well," Pasha said. "May I get you some refreshments? Tea, perhaps?"

"That would be nice," Faye said.

"Very well," Pasha said, putting his hands together, and giving a little bow. Then he backed out of the room.

"This place is like a museum," Mystery said as she examined the dusty contents of the shelves. "I can see why Father would have been drawn to this place."

"Yes," Faye said.

"Look at this," Mystery said as she picked up a drinking goblet that had been made from a human skull mounted on a silver base. The skull was upside down and had been cut in two about the line of the upper jaw, so that the open cranium formed the cup of the goblet. The eye sockets and the nasal cavities were filled with hammered gold. The skull had been bleached and polished to an ivorylike degree of brightness, although the teeth were somewhat yellow. One of the molars was capped with gold.

"Is it real?" she asked.

Indy took it. The inside of the cranium was etched with the rivulets for blood vessels that, in life, had helped supply blood to the brain.

"I'm afraid so," Indy said.

"Yuck," Mystery said. She made a face and wiped the palms of her hands on her jeans. "Who could be so twisted as to want to drink from a human skull?"

"It is used for ritual magic," Indy said. "Common among primitive peoples all over the world. The idea is that if you make your rival's head into a cup, then each time you drink from it you are symbolically ingesting his power. Surely it's just a piece of the collection."

Faye took the goblet from Indy.

"Among some tribes, it is a symbol of respect, even veneration," she said. "The greater your enemy, the greater therefore you must be."

"How barbaric," Mystery said.

"Hmm," Faye said. "It's not dusty like the other items."

"You can't be suggesting . . . ," Indy said.

Faye wiped the interior of the cranium with her middle finger, then tasted it.

"Wine," she said. "White. Not too old, I'd say."

"Terrific," Indy said.

Faye placed the goblet back on the shelf.

"Let's hope," she said, "that the owner of this skull was already dead before Jadoo fancied his head as a drinking cup."

"I wonder if *he* had an appointment," Indy said.

"We'll ask," Faye said.

Pasha returned with a tray. He poured strong British tea from a silver kettle into three cups. Faye took the steaming cup that was offered, but Indy declined.

"Me neither," said Mystery.

"Oh?" Pasha asked. "Could I get the young lady some milk, and the gentleman some wine, perhaps?"

Mystery shook her head.

"No thanks," Indy said with a smile. "I'm not thirsty."

"As you wish," Pasha said. "I expect the master back shortly. In the meantime, is there anything else that I could get for your comfort?"

"Actually, there is," Indy said. "We're expecting

a wire from the States this afternoon. Could you telephone the Western Union office and ask them to deliver it here?"

"We have no telephone," Pasha said. "But I will send a messenger to the telegraph office. In whose name will this message be directed?"

"Mine," Indy said.

"Very well, Dr. Jones."

Indy searched Pasha's eyes, but he did not flinch.

"You must have a phenomenal memory," Indy said.

"Beg your pardon, sir?"

"I don't remember telling you that I was a professor."

"We do receive newswire reports, even in Calcutta," Pasha said. "It would be a very uninformed citizen of the empire who did not know the name of the famous archaeologist."

Pasha backed out of the room.

"You don't trust him," Faye said.

"There's not many people I *do* trust," Indy said. Then, when he felt Mystery's eyes on the back of his neck he added: "Present company excepted."

There was the sound of a closing door somewhere nearby, and hushed voices followed by approaching footsteps. A tall, white-haired man wearing a black turban and jacket entered the room.

His skin was the color of walnut, but his eyes were a piercing blue.

"Guests," he said. "Forgive me for making you wait. Had I known you were here, I would have hurried. Please, come into my inner office."

"Thank you," Faye said.

They followed him into a dark, well-carpeted room where a ceiling fan turned slowly. The magician sat in a richly upholstered chair and withdrew a cigar from a wooden box on a side table, then offered the box to Indy.

"No thanks," Indy said. "I don't smoke."

"I do," Faye said.

"As you wish," Jadoo said and allowed her to select a cigar.

Jadoo lit his cigar with a wooden match, then passed the matches to Faye. She bit off one end of the cigar, then sucked flame into the other end of it.

"I didn't know you smoked, Mother."

"I've had to give it up," Faye said as the smoke serpentined around her head, drawn upward by the ceiling fan. "It's difficult to get American cigarettes, and the local stuff they smoke stinks too much. My, this is strong."

Jadoo smiled.

"Dr. Jones, I know you by reputation. And madam, Pasha tells me that you are the wife of my peer, Kaspar Maskelyne. How may I help you?"

"It is because of my husband that we are here," Faye said. "We've been told that he may have visited you before his disappearance, some four years ago."

Jadoo puffed on his cigar.

"Yes," he said. "Of course I remember him. He spent the day with me, in 1930, I believe. He has disappeared? I am sorry to hear that."

"We were hoping," Indy said, "that you could share with us the substance of your conversation with him, to better inform our search."

"Ah, it was so long ago," Jadoo said. "And, I am sorry to admit, my memory is not what it once was. What strikes me most about the conversation now is how pleasant it was. We discussed the history of magic, of course, and he took notes for a book he said he was writing."

"A book?" Faye asked. "He never told me about a book."

"Now, let me think," Jadoo said and closed his eyes. "It does seem to me that a book was involved in the discussion. We talked of so many things."

"Kaspar was not the type to attempt a book," Faye said. "He was more the adventurer than the scholar. In fact, I only received three letters from him before his disappearance, and those were maddeningly brief. I have wished many times that he had been more inclined to document his activities, because it would have made the search for him that much easier."

"Now I remember," Jadoo said. "He was not writing a book about ancient magic, but looking for one. I was not familiar with it, because it seemed to deal more with religion than magic."

"Did you have any advice for him?" Indy asked.

"Yes. He asked me about ancient Hindu texts, and I was able to tell him something about Sanskrit. We also talked of the nearly universal belief among the world's religions of a book or tablet which contains the histories of every person who will ever live."

"The Omega Book," Faye said.

"That is what some cultures call it," Jadoo said. "The ancient Egyptians, for example, believed that in the city of Heliopolis, near Cairo, there was a great sacred pillar named Annu that stood before civilization existed, and contained secret knowledge on 36,535 scrolls hidden inside. The knowledge could only be revealed to the worthy, and for the benefit of the world."

Indy laughed. "That's a metaphor," he said. "The 36,535 scrolls represent the 365 days of the year, plus a fraction of the day, and there are some interpretations that the knowledge is not contained within the pillar, but in the sky—in other words, the stars."

"As above, so below," Jadoo said, quoting a common occult saying. "Plato supposedly visited the temple of Neith, where there were secret halls containing historical records which had been kept for more than nine thousand years. The historian Manetho, who provided the chronology of pharaohs and dynasties that is still used today, is said to have extracted his history from certain pillars which he discovered in underground places, upon which Hermes had inscribed the sacred letters."

"I've heard the myths," Indy said. "Including that of Edgar Cayce, the so-called sleeping prophet, who predicted that a 'Hall of Records' that contains the history of a lost civilization would be discovered beneath the paws of the Sphinx."

"Of course," Jadoo said. "We also talked of some of the great archaeological finds, and how many of them seemed more to do with magic than science. It is amazing, isn't it, how many discoveries involve three persons—a rogue archaeologist, his sponsor, and a teenaged daughter of one of the principals?"

"The Tomb of Tutankhamen," Indy said, "or the Crystal Skull of Lubantuun."

"Precisely," Jadoo said. "Surely there is some mysterious power at work there that science can never fully comprehend. After all, luck plays such a tremendous part in the act of digging in the earth, does it not?"

"In your conversation with Kaspar about this ancient book," Indy asked, "was there mention of using anything other than luck to find it?"

"Yes," Jadoo said. "The Staff of Aaron."

"Why did Kaspar believe the Staff would help him find these records?" Indy asked. "We're dealing with unrelated theologies."

"Because the Staff can find anything," Jadoo said. "It helped the Israelites find water in the desert, for example; strike a rock with it, and a spring flowed. Kaspar believed that such divine intervention was necessary to find the right spot to dig in the sand. After all, it is something like attempting to find a needle in a haystack, as you Americans say."

"Belief in the Staff is traditional in Islam, Judaism, and Christianity," Indy said. "Aaron was supposedly 123 years old when he died and was buried at Mount Hor. As to the final location of his staff, the texts are silent."

"Not all texts," Jadoo said.

"You have some information you'd like to share?"

Jadoo shrugged.

"Chasing rumors and folklore is like trying to catch the wind," he said. "But there is a persistent tale of the Staff still being worshiped by a tribe of devil worshipers in Iraq called the Yezidi."

"Devil worshipers?" Mystery asked. "Why would they worship something that is so connected with the biblical story of Exodus?"

"Because Aaron and his sister, a sorceress named Miriam, lost their faith while their brother Moses was on the mountain receiving the Ten Commandments from God," Indy said. "They urged the Israelites to construct the Golden Calf and to worship it."

"The Yezidi are an unusual people," Jadoo said. "They are located in a remote mountain area to the north of Baghdad, and foreigners are strictly forbidden to go there. I told Kaspar that he had better be careful if he reached them, because they anger easily and are not responsive to reason. What is the American expression? They would as soon slit your throat as look at you."

"So Kaspar was planning to go to Iraq?"

"Yes, I believe that was his plan," Jadoo said. "But I don't know, because I never heard from him after. Neither did he discuss his route with me."

"Thank you," Faye said as she knocked the ashes of her cigar into a tray. "You have given us our first real clue to my husband's whereabouts."

"I only wish I could be more specific," Jadoo said apologetically.

"I have one more question," Faye asked.

"Certainly," Jadoo said.

"There is a goblet made from a human skull in your collection in the next room," she said. "We observed that it was not dusty, like the other pieces, and it smelled of wine."

"Ah," Jadoo said and smiled. "You were wondering if, true to my name, I take refreshment from it. No, I'm sorry to disappoint you. I acquired that relic some years ago in Tibet, and through neglect a family of mice came to nest inside it. When I discovered it last week, I asked Pasha to clean it. He used vinegar, which accounts for the odor."

"That explains it," Faye said.

"What do you mean, 'true to your name'?" Mystery asked.

The magician looked uncomfortable.

"Jadoo," Indy explained, "means 'black magic.' "

"A stage affectation," the magician said.

There was a rap at the door, and Pasha entered. He was carrying a tray, and there was a heavy yellow piece of paper on it, folded so as to make it its own envelope.

"Excuse me," he said. "A message for Dr. Jones."

"Thank you," Indy said.

Indy opened the telegram and read it.

"It's from Marcus Brody," he said, and his voice nearly cracked. "He says that he is distressed to learn that I'm in India instead of China, but that he has directed a transfer of funds to the British Mercantile Bank here. All I have to do is go to the bank and give our usual code word."

"You seem surprised to hear from your old friend," Faye said.

"Not surprised," Indy said. "Simply nostalgic."

"You have a code word?" Mystery asked.

"Yes," Indy said proudly. "A mnemonic device we agreed upon, something from childhood. It certainly comes in handy."

"But what if somebody guesses it?" she asked.

"Oh, that won't happen," he said. "The word is part of a sequence, which progresses each time we use it. Oh, no."

"Dr. Jones," Faye said. "What's wrong? You look suddenly ill."

"I can't remember where we are in the sequence," he stammered.

"All right, Dr. Jones," the banker said cheerfully. "My name is Mr. Hyde, and I will be overseeing the funds transfer from America. One thousand American dollars."

They were sitting in a well-appointed office of the British Mercantile Bank, while Faye and Mystery waited in the lobby outside. The banker had seemed somewhat alarmed at Indy's disheveled condition,

and had insisted that he leave the whip and the gun
with Faye.

"Terrific," Indy said. "You don't know what a
help this is."

"Sign this, please."

He pushed a form across to Indy.

Indy signed it and dated it, then handed it back.

"The date," the banker said.

"What? Oh, sorry. I'm always behind when the
year changes."

"You are a quarter of a century ahead," the
banker observed.

"There's a funny story behind that," Indy said.

"I'm sure there is," the banker said without emotion. "Now, do you have some identification? Your
passport will do."

"I'm sorry, I don't," Indy said.

"You're traveling without a passport?"

"I lost it in the storm that sank our ship," Indy
said.

"Something else, then. A birth certificate?"

"That's not something I normally carry with me."

"A library card, perhaps."

"I told you," Indy said. His eyes glistened and his
cheeks were beginning to redden. "I lost everything
in the typhoon. We are in a desperate situation here,
or I wouldn't be wiring my friend Marcus Brody for
money."

"All right, Dr. Jones, no need to get angry," Hyde said. "There is one last recourse here. I just need to verify your identity with the code word which Mr. Brody has given us."

Indy grinned.

"Another funny story," he said.

"I'll take your word for it," the banker said.

"Can I give you the entire phrase, of which—"

"The code word, Dr. Jones," the banker insisted.

Indy mumbled.

"I beg your pardon?"

"Boy," Indy said.

"No, I'm sorry."

"Does."

"Quite wrong."

"Fine," Indy said.

"Well," the banker said.

"That's it," Indy said. "I couldn't remember which note we used last. Every Good Boy Does Fine. The phrase stands for the lines of the great musical staff, and we used D last time."

The banker looked at him suspiciously.

"Look, I've just given you the code," he said. "Wire Brody if you must and ask him to confirm it—we'll have to change it now, anyway."

"Wait here, please," the banker said. "I'll get the money for you."

The banker left the office and Indy waited

nervously. When the man returned, he was accompanied by a bank security guard.

"What's wrong?" Indy asked.

"You're under arrest for fraud," Hyde said. "The correct response was, 'Every.' "

"You're making a big mistake," Indy said.

"I'm afraid not, Dr. Jones—or whoever you are," Hyde said. "Our description for Professor Jones is of a man considerably younger than yourself. He would certainly have no gray in his hair. In addition, Mr. Brody told us that he believed you were in South America. We must conclude, therefore, that you are an impostor attempting to assume the identity of Dr. Jones in order to make some quick cash from Mr. Brody's museum."

"Get Marcus on the phone," Indy said. "Let me talk to him."

"That is quite impossible," Hyde said.

"Please," Indy said. "You don't understand."

"I'm afraid we do," Hyde said. "You will be held by the Calcutta police until we can sort this thing out."

"Behave yourself," the guard told him while he handcuffed Indy's hands behind his back. "There's a good fellow. No use struggling."

As Indy was led away through the lobby, Faye called out to him.

"Where are they taking you?" she asked.

"The Calcutta jail," Indy said. "They think I'm trying to rob them. They don't believe I'm me."

"You're making a mistake," Faye told them. "This is Dr. Jones."

"This bloke apparently has you fooled as well," the guard said. "How do you know he is Dr. Jones?"

"Because he told us he was."

"How long have you known him?"

"A few days," she said.

"You lied?" Mystery asked.

"No," Indy said.

"Do you have any other proof?" the guard asked.

"Well, no," Faye said. "But I trust him."

"Begging your pardon," the guard said. "But there's your first mistake, madam. I'm sorry, but I'm going to have to take you and the girl in for questioning as well. Let me have the gun."

"Indy," Faye said. "What do you want me to do?"

"Hand it to him," Indy said.

She gave the guard the holstered Webley. He tucked it under his arm, then drew a second and third pair of handcuffs from his back pocket.

"Since there's only one of me and three of you," he said apologetically as he held up the additional sets of cuffs, "the bloke here will go to jail, but you women will be released after the inspectors have a chance to question you."

"Let them go," Indy said.

"Sorry, mate."

The guard handcuffed Mystery's hands behind her back, then turned to her mother. Mystery was out of the cuffs in a few seconds, and she snatched the Webley from beneath his arm.

"I've had enough of this," Mystery said as she unholstered the revolver and pointed it at the bank guard.

"Now, miss," the guard said. "You could hurt somebody with that."

"That's the point," she said. "I'm not letting you take Dr. Jones. You know what they call the jail here? The black hole. People go in and never come out. Let him go."

"All right," the guard said and released Indy.

"Let's get out of here," Mystery said.

Indy took the gun from the guard's holster.

"Not yet," Indy said. "I'll have that money now, Mr. Hyde."

"You're robbing me?"

"No," Indy said. "That thousand dollars really is meant for me. It's not your money, it's Marcus Brody's—or at least his museum's."

"Very well," Hyde said. "It will take a moment."

"I don't care if it's in dollars, pounds, or rupees,"

Indy said. "Just hurry. And don't try anything, because we're desperate."

"Right," Mystery said.

"Give me that," Faye said and took the gun from
her. "You're not going to shoot anybody."

"*Faye,*" Indy said. "This is kind of a delicate situation. Would you please not undermine our position?"

"I won't be having my daughter waving guns
around," she said.

"Fine," Indy said. "Then you wave it."

Hyde came back with the money, which was
in pounds. Indy stuffed it in his jacket and tipped
his hat.

"Remember," he said. "We only took what was
mine."

Then all three ran for the door.

Sokai was still unaccustomed to the black silk patch
over his eye, and he tilted his head back at an awkward angle as he looked at the old magician. Sokai,
who was wearing a white suit beneath his black
trench coat, lit an American cigarette and crossed
his legs while Jadoo fidgeted with a cigar.

Musashi stood behind Sokai's chair.

"This man Jones," Sokai said simply. "Tell me
what you know of him."

"He was here," Jadoo said. "And his two companions. A woman by the name of Maskelyne and her daughter. They should be well on their way to Baghdad by now."

"What did they want?" Sokai asked.

"They were searching for clues to the woman's missing husband," Jadoo said. "I told them that he was here, four years ago."

"Go on," Sokai said.

"I led them to believe that I was sympathetic to their search."

"Yes," Sokai said. "What else?"

"Jones received a telegram from New York. Money was waiting for him at the British Mercantile Bank."

"That will make him harder to catch," Sokai said.

"Why do you want him?"

"Personal reasons," Sokai said and touched the eye patch. "Also, they search for something which interests me. Why are they on their way to Baghdad?"

"Because I told them the husband believed he would find the Rod of Aaron among the Yezidi of northern Iraq," Jadoo said. "That much is true."

"But they won't find the husband there," Sokai said.

"No," Jadoo said.

"Why have you never sought this fabled rod, if the husband shared its location with you?"

"Because the Yezidi are not a tribe I am anxious to visit," Jadoo said. "I have never been inclined to risk my life for an uncertain reward."

"Ah," Sokai said, "but what if someone else does the real work by locating the prize first?"

"Then it would be a prize for the taking," Jadoo said.

Sokai laughed.

"We seem to share compatible philosophies," Sokai said. "Let us join forces to bring about the destruction of Jones and his companions. We will have what is his."

"We've got a problem," Indy said as he sat down between Faye and Mystery in the crowded railcar bound for the heart of the Indian subcontinent. The conductor had punched their tickets without so much as a second glance.

"Other than being fugitives?" Mystery asked.

"Keep your voice down," Indy said. "No, I think we're safe now. The problem is that once we get to the Pakistani border—a week from now, or two weeks, depending on our luck and the whims of the Indian railway system—the rails end."

"All right," Faye said. "Then we hire a driver."

"There are no roads," Indy said. "At least not in the modern sense of the word. There are nothing but goat paths, switchbacks, and unmarked graves for fifteen hundred miles of rocks and desert. The two countries between us and Baghdad, Pakistan and Iran, belong more to the Middle Ages than to the twentieth century."

"So how do people cross it?" Mystery asked.

"Generally, they don't," Indy said. "When they have to, they go in caravans, just like they did a thousand years ago on the old Silk Road."

"Then we'll find a caravan," Faye said.

"It takes six weeks to cross that much desert on a camel," Indy said. "I don't know about you, but I don't think I can spare the time—or the trouble. Have you ever ridden a camel?"

"No," Faye said.

"It's miserable," Indy said. "The smell alone is enough to drive you nuts. But if our timing is right, and our money holds out, we can rent a plane from one of the oil companies. If we're lucky, we might even find a plane that can still fly for more than fifty miles at a hop. The desert is notoriously hard on aircraft."

"So," Mystery asked. "Is that the plan?"

"Yes, Dr. Jones," Faye said. "What is our next move?"

"The smart move would be to go home," Indy suggested.

"Home," Faye said, "is where my husband is."

"Look, Faye," Indy said. "You have nothing left to prove. Nobody would blame you if you gave up, declared him officially missing in action, and went on with your life. I'm sorry, but that's the size of it."

"You just don't get it, do you?" Faye asked.

"Get what?" Indy said.

"We have to know," Faye said. "If he's alive, I want to find him. If he's dead, I can deal with that. But either way, I have to know—it's this purgatory of not knowing that I can't tolerate. If you're not going to help, then Mystery and I will do it by ourselves."

Indy clenched his jaw and looked away.

"You seem to be forgetting something, Dr. Jones."

"Oh? What's that?" Indy snapped.

"The long shot that Kaspar actually found the Staff of Aaron, and perhaps the Omega Book. You may be right, Dr. Jones: Kaspar may have died long ago. But his cold dead fingers may be clutching the Staff of Aaron, which in turn points to the Omega Book. It would be the greatest archaeological find and treasure trove of our age. Imagine, Dr. Jones. Your career could come into the daylight. You would no longer be forced to rob graves in the dead of night while dodging goons with machine guns."

"I like my work," Indy said defensively.

"Who wouldn't?" Faye asked. "You get to travel and meet new people with interesting and usually sadistic hobbies. When's the last time you brought anything of real value back to your museum in New York?"

Indy coughed.

"There were several items from Qin's tomb that were quite nice," he said softly. "And I've had other adventures, but I can't talk about most of them. Nobody would believe me, anyway."

"So what's one more adventure," Faye continued, "just one more shot at the jackpot. You know you can't resist."

"All right," Indy said as he rubbed his hand over his stubbled jaw. "We'll keep pushing on—keep hoping for the best, but expecting the worst. And one other thing: Since we will be sharing hardships equally on this expedition, we will also share equally in whatever *rewards* are unearthed. Agreed?"

"Agreed, Dr. Jones." Then Faye paused. "With the provision, of course, that if I should not survive . . . Mystery will receive my full cut, and you will do your best to see her back safely to Oklahoma."

"I could do no less," Indy said.

"I can take care of myself, you old fossil,"

Mystery said as she batted Indy's fedora from his head. "As for Mother, she is just as capable as I, and nothing is going to happen to her. But in the unlikely event that it does, Dr. Jones, I will hold you personally responsible for making me an orphan."

7

CHILDREN OF THE DEVIL

The big silver biplane with the red Standard Oil logo emblazoned on its corrugated sides glided down to within a yard or two of the desert floor. The 360-horsepower Wright radial engine sputtered and died as it sucked the last drop of fuel from the ninety-gallon tank. The big low-pressure tires bounced twice on the hardpan, leaving twin plumes of dust behind, and then there was a jolt as the tail wheel dropped to the deck.

Sitting on the floor of the cargo hold of the PT6 transport, Faye Maskelyne lost her balance and nearly landed in Indy's lap.

"Sorry," she mumbled, suddenly self-conscious.

When the aircraft had rolled to a stop, Mystery unlatched the rear cargo door and jumped down to the ground. Both she and her mother were dressed in khakis they'd purchased two weeks earlier at a bazaar in an unnamed village along the banks of the Indus.

The Iraqi sun blazed overhead, and with the exception of some hazy blue mountains in the north, there was nothing to see except the unforgiving desert.

"Where are we?" Mystery asked.

"Somewhere in the Upper Plain," Indy said as he emerged from the plane with a plank of wood. "Here—position this on the ground, would you?"

Indy mounted one of the two motorcycles in the cargo bay, released the clutch, and rolled it down the board to the ground. Then he returned to the aircraft and did the same thing with the other motorcycle, which had a sidecar attached.

Both motorcycles were red American-made Indians, and both had already been well-used by the time Indy had spent the last of the money to buy them from a trader at the oil company camp in the Pakistani desert the day before. The first motorcycle was a 1929 Indian 4, with four black exhaust pipes exiting on the left side and a broad seat that looked like it belonged on a tractor. The motorcycle with the sidecar was a 1928 Scout. On the sidecar was painted, in English and Arabic, *Property of British Geologic Survey.*

Faye brought out the food and supplies, which they strapped to the motorcycles and packed into the luggage area of the sidecar. They hung the canvas water bags from the front fenders of the bikes.

Indy and Mystery then hauled out the gasoline, ten cans of which were designated to get the aircraft back to the Indian border. The other eight cans would be strapped to the rears of the motorcycles.

The pilot opened the big triangular glass-paned door and jumped down from the cockpit.

"You cut that a little close, didn't you?" Indy asked.

"This was the first flat spot I could find that wasn't strewn with rocks," the pilot said. "Besides, you said you wanted to get as close to Lalesh as possible. Well, it's about a hundred miles in that direction."

The pilot jerked his thumb over his shoulder to the north.

After they had finished refueling the aircraft, Indy took the map from his satchel and unfolded it on the ground, then placed his compass on it.

"Okay," he said, sitting on his haunches. "The Tigris River is due west, the mountains are to the northeast, and you say Lalesh is a hundred miles north. That would place us about here."

Indy jabbed the map with his index finger.

"A little more over here, I think," the pilot said.

"All right," Indy said. "If we average thirty miles an hour across the desert, we should reach Lalesh by nightfall. If there anything in particular we should know?"

"Iraq is a British protectorate," the pilot said, "but up here on the Upper Plain you're on your own. Iraq does have its own army, but I wouldn't trust them if you meet them; the officers tend to lean toward fascism and they are busy brewing up a war with the British. They won't be fond of Americans. Stay away from the Yezidi tribes, because they have a nasty reputation."

"I've heard," Indy said.

"Baghdad is around three hundred miles to the south," the pilot said. "If you get lost, just find the Tigris River and follow it down. Also, there should be a couple of British oil company outposts where you can buy fuel on the way back."

Indy folded the map and put it back in his pocket.

"Thanks," he said as he stood and shook the pilot's hand.

"This is the first time I've flown somebody out to the middle of nowhere and dropped them off," the pilot said. "Good luck, because I know you'll need it."

Indy mounted the Indian 4 while Faye and Mystery argued over who was going to ride in the sidecar. They finally agreed to flip a coin for it, and Mystery won; she climbed into the Scout's saddle while her mother took the sidecar.

"Do you now how to ride that thing?" Indy asked as he slipped on his goggles.

Mystery just smiled at him and kicked the starter. The Scout's engines puttered to life, and then the rear wheel skidded in the dust as she dumped the clutch and twisted the throttle.

"Hey!" he shouted. "That bike has to last us several hundred miles. There are no garages out here!"

Mystery, however, could not hear him.

"Kids," Indy said and shook his head.

Then he started his own bike and followed.

For an hour they rode across the plateau, occasionally steering around boulders or climbing a gully, their dust trails hanging behind them in the hot afternoon air.

Indy checked the compass often to make sure they were still headed in the right direction. They stopped once for lunch, then Faye and Mystery switched places and they pressed onward. As the afternoon wore on, the terrain became rougher, and they found themselves approaching a high mound overlooking the Tigris River. At the apex of the mound was a group of ancient ruins, some of which had obviously been excavated in the not-so-distant past.

Indy brought his motorcycle to a stop and Mystery pulled up beside him.

"What is this?" Faye asked.

"Nineveh," Indy said. "One of the oldest cities in the world, supposedly founded by Nimrod, great-grandson of Noah. It was destroyed by the Babylonians in the sixth century before Christ."

"Where to now?" Faye asked.

"There's an ancient road that leads from here to the mountains in the northeast," Indy said. "We take it."

The road was little more than a goat path, and it was so rough that they were forced to reduce their speed to nearly a crawl for fear of breaking the springs of the motorcycles. Totally intent on negotiating the road, Indy did not notice that they had been followed for the last ten miles.

Suddenly there were four riders on each side of them, and they easily kept pace with the motorcycles. The horses were white Arabians, sixteen hands high, and the riders wore dark robes and carried ancient muzzle-loading rifles. From their belts hung *khanjers,* the wicked-looking curved daggers of the desert.

On flat ground the vehicles could have easily outrun them, but not here. Indy throttled down his motorcycle and brought it smoothly to a stop, and Faye did the same.

"Don't make any sudden moves," Indy said with a smile, looking at the riders but talking to Mystery and Faye. "And whatever you do, don't speak to them, because that would be an insult. Only men speak to men."

The leader was a big man with bright blue eyes that peered from a face as weathered as the landscape around them. His nose was like one of the larger boulders, and his hair and beard were the color and texture of steel wool.

He jumped down from his horse and approached Indy. He had his flintlock rifle in the crook of his left arm, and his right hand was free to wield the *khanjer* if needed.

He greeted Indy in Arabic, then said:

"I speak English a little."

"Good," Indy said, and he drew back his jacket a little so the holstered Webley would be evident. "I speak Arabic a little."

"I am Sheikh Ali Azhad."

"My name is Dr. Jones," Indy said in Arabic, knowing how much stock this part of the world put in titles. "These women are my assistants. They are unimportant, but I am fond of them. They are mine."

Faye smiled pleasantly, unaware of the conversation.

The sheikh nodded.

"You treat sick people?" he asked.

"No," Indy said. "I'm not that kind of a doctor—I'm a teacher, an archaeologist. I dig in the ground."

"What do you look for?" the sheikh asked.

"The past," Indy said.

The sheikh nodded gravely.

"We have been waiting three days for you," he said. "In a dream I saw you coming, upon your red machines. All three of you. But I thought you were three men. I was fooled, because your women wear pants. That is the way of dreams. They are true, but you do not know in which way until it comes to pass."

"You are Yezidi?" Indy asked. "You live in Lalesh?"

"We call it Sheikh Adda, in honor of our great prophet. It lies in the valley, yonder. We are a peaceful people. The world does not understand us. They try to kill us, to wipe us out. Why are you here?"

"The dream did not tell you?" Indy asked, gambling.

The sheikh grunted.

"May I see your gun?"

Indy took the Webley from the holster and extended it toward the Sheikh butt-first.

"If I can see yours," he said.

The sheikh handed him the flintlock and took the Webley.

The rifle was old, perhaps a hundred years or more, but well cared for. It smelled of oil and black gunpowder. It was of about forty caliber, and a fresh flint was in the hammer.

The sheikh opened the cylinder of the Webley, noted the brass cartridges, closed the revolver, and tested its heft by sighting on a mountain peak. Then he returned it to Indy, and Indy handed him the rifle.

"Very nice," Indy said.

The sheikh nodded in satisfaction.

"I call you Jones."

Indy nodded.

"I'll call you Ali," he said.

"I take you to Sheikh Adda," Ali said. "But first, rules: No spitting. No wearing blue. No making Shaitan angry."

The sheikh mounted his horse and led the way down the road, followed by the other seven riders. Indy started his motorcycle.

"Who's Shaitan?" Faye asked.

"Satan," Indy said.

The village of Sheikh Adda, the holiest of the Yezidi cities, was a collection of white, cone-shaped tombs and temples in the center of a few hundred huts situated in a green valley. Peacocks, symbols of one of the semideities that the Yezidi believed ruled the earth, roamed freely. There appeared to be little commerce other than the raising of goats and horses, and by Yezidi standards Ali was a wealthy man because he owned a gun, a horse, a *khanjer,* and his own little shop that dealt in tea and the cheapest of Western trinkets. Because he was considered the most powerful man in the village, other than the high priest, he had been allowed to learn and speak English.

"How many Yezidi are there?" Mystery asked as she got out of the sidecar.

"Nobody knows," Indy said. "Estimates range from a few thousand to perhaps tens of thousands. In an area in which religious war is the biggest industry, the Yezidi have the misfortune of being identified with the one personality that is nearly universally hated. They have been persecuted for centuries."

"How long have they been around?"

"Nobody knows that, either," Indy said. "But they appear to be one of the oldest religious groups in the world. Some have claimed they are a direct link to the religion of the Sumerians, but that hasn't been proven. They can be traced as far back as the mystery religions, however."

"Do they really worship the devil?" she asked.

"Worship is the wrong word," Ali told Indy as he approached. It would have been impolite for him to answer Mystery directly. "We believe that Allah is good. Because Allah is good, we have nothing to fear from Him. It is Shaitan you must watch out for and give respect."

"What are the ways in which you give respect?" Indy asked.

"In every aspect of life, of course," Ali said. "Come, are you hungry? We will eat."

Indy followed Ali into his house, but stopped Faye and Mystery before they could enter.

"Sorry," he said. "But you have to wait out here until the men finish. Then, you'll be brought the scraps."

"The *scraps*?" Mystery asked.

"She's right," Faye said. "That's barbaric."

"Don't make a scene," Indy said. "It reflects badly on me. Look, I don't make the rules around here. Besides, it could be worse; at least you don't have to wear veils, which is considered pretty progressive in this part of the world. If you're hungry, there is plenty of decent chow in the sidecar."

After the meal, Indy emerged wearing a white turban and a coarse *zebun*, the traditional Arab homespun robe. Over his arm were a pair of dark robes. He paused just outside the hut, put his hands on his stomach, and belched elaborately.

Faye and Mystery were still sitting beside the motorcycles, since none of the other villagers, male or female, dared to express the slightest interest in them.

Ali slapped Indy on the back and thanked him for the compliment. "Come," he said. "I will show you your house. Bring your women."

"Have a good time?" Faye asked.

"You got the best end of the stick, believe me," Indy whispered. "Mutton and sheep eyes. I'd give anything for a ham sandwich right now."

"Sorry," Faye said. "Mysti and I ate all the potted ham."

"It was delicious," Mystery said.

"Here, put these on," Indy said as he threw the robes at Faye. "They think it's indecent for a woman to wear pants."

Ali led them to a modest hut not far from the village well. They left the motorcycles outside, after Indy removed the spark plug wires.

"Don't you trust us?" Ali asked.

"Of course," Indy said as he stuffed the plug wires into his satchel. "But would you leave your horse outside with a bit still between his teeth?"

The dirt floor of the hut had been freshly raked,

and there were two straw mats arranged for sleeping. Other than the mats, there was no furniture. A basket of fruit had been placed by the doorway, which was covered with a strip of canvas.

"I hope you find it adequate," Ali said.

"More than adequate," Indy said. "Thank you, my friend."

Before dawn the next morning, Ali crept inside the hut and knelt beside Indy. Faye and her daughter were still asleep, sharing a straw mat in the far corner of the hut.

Ali placed a hand on his shoulder.

Indy's eyes snapped open, and his hand reached for his revolver. Ali's *khanjer* was at his throat before Indy's fingers could close around the butt of the Webley.

"It is only I," Ali said as he sheathed the knife.

"I thought somebody was trying to steal the bikes," Indy said, lowering the revolver.

"Dress quickly, my friend," Ali said. "Here, put on this turban—the proper headgear for a man. You have been invited to our temple, something no white man has seen before—at least not one who has lived to tell about it."

"Why me?" Indy asked as he pulled on his boots.

"Because of my dream," Ali said, "and because

the other sheikhs attach significance to your visit as well. This is a time of great portent."

Indy followed Ali outside as he wrapped the turban around his head. The stars were shining brightly in a cloudless sky. They walked down the dirt street to the temple with the cone-shaped top, and Ali paused. A dozen pairs of shoes and boots were outside the doorway.

"Take off your boots," he told Indy. "Leave them outside, and do not step on the threshold when you cross the doorway. Say nothing, do nothing, unless you are instructed."

Once inside the temple, Ali took a lighted candle from a table and moved a tapestry hanging on the far side of the rounded wall, revealing a flight of stairs. *Khanjer* in hand, a priest stood beside the tapestry, which represented a peacock.

"Is this always guarded?" Indy asked.

"Of course," Ali said as he descended the steps. "This is the center of worship for all Yezidi. It is ancient beyond memory. We cannot allow you to witness our rituals, but as sheikh I can show you our most venerated object. After all, that is why you are here, is it not?"

Indy smiled, but said nothing.

On the walls of the passage were representations of large black snakes twisted around each other.

Indy could hear the sound of running water, and as they descended the sound grew louder.

"What do the pictures of the snakes mean?"

Ali held his finger to his lips.

When they reached the bottom of the steps, they were in a large granite cavern. Ali used the candle to light a pair of torches held in sconces upon the wall. In the center of the room was a pit, and at the bottom of the pit was a flowing stream of clear water.

"You may ask questions about anything except the pictures upon the wall," Ali said. "Those are the property of Shaitan, and we are forbidden to speak of them."

"The water," Indy said. "It is from the village well."

"Yes," Ali said. "Our temples are always built over underground streams."

Then Ali walked over to an alcove cut into the rock, and from the light of his candle Indy could see the wooden doors of a coffin-shaped reliquary.

Ali opened the doors, revealing a bone-white piece of wood. It was nearly two meters long, Indy judged. Ali gently removed the Staff from its resting place.

"You may hold it," Ali said, "but under no circumstances it is allowed to touch the floor."

Indy nodded, then took the Staff.

"It is so light," Indy said.

"It is very old, and has lost much of its weight. If you were to drop it, it would shatter like a piece of glass."

"Bring the candle closer," Indy said. "there are some markings here, but I cannot make them out. They look like Hebrew, but I can't be sure."

"It has not produced miracles in my lifetime," Ali said. "It has healed the sick in the past. I remember my grandfather telling me about the lepers and the demon-possessed it cured."

"Is that why you thought I was a physician?"

"More of a hope, really," Ali said. "We have had a few foreigners come seeking the Staff every generation or so, but they are always after power."

"Within the last few years," Indy asked, "was there ever an Englishman named Kaspar?"

"No," Ali said. "You are the first in a generation."

"The Staff and the . . . ," Indy said and nodded toward the stairway. "We have a Western symbol, the caduceus, which represents healing, that is a combination of those pictures and the Staff."

"I know of it," Ali said.

"How did the Staff come into the possession of your people?"

"We do not really know," Ali said. "there is an old story about the Staff and the Ark of the

Covenant being stolen from Solomon's Temple at the same time, long ago, but we cannot be sure. It is just a story."

Indy carefully handed the Staff back to Ali, and as the sheikh put it back into the reliquary Indy asked:

"Has anyone asked merely to borrow the Staff?"

"That would be quite impossible," Ali said. "We have very strict laws about that. It must remain here, under our protection. And if someone were to steal it, woe to them. After we cut off their hands, they would be staked in the desert and disemboweled. What a feast for the vultures, eh? But we are a peaceful people. Tell me, Dr. Jones, what is your interest in the Staff?"

"Purely academic," Indy said.

"Of course," Ali said. "You know, there is one circumstance only in which the Staff may leave the village, and that is in the hands of the Expected One, who again can bring forth miracles with the aid of the Staff. Frankly, my friend, I was hoping that would be you."

"I'm not your man," Indy said. "Sorry."

"So am I," Ali said. "We are sorely in need of the Age of Miracles to return. In my dream, even the heavens responded to the will of the Chosen One."

* * *

"So you saw it," Faye said.

They were sitting on the straw mats in the hut, and Indy had just finished telling her about the tour of the temple and its underground chamber.

"Yes, or something like it," Indy said. "Very old, kept in a wooden cabinet in an alcove cut into the rock."

"This pit that had the well water in it," Mystery said. "How big was it?"

"About three feet across."

"Could you tell how deep the water was, or the chamber in which it ran?"

"No," Indy said, "it was too dark."

"This is going to be difficult," Faye said.

"This is impossible," Indy said. "The temple is guarded around the clock."

"Yes, but just by one priest," Faye said.

"There's no way to get past him. Even if you could somehow overpower him, you'd have to fight the entire village to escape."

"Maybe," Faye said. "Unless you could put a duplicate in its place. From your description, it doesn't sound all that special-looking."

"Look, I don't want to have my hands chopped off and then be staked in the desert to serve as food for vultures," Indy said. "It's just too risky. And besides that, it wouldn't be right. These people have shared their food and their shelter with us. Let's not repay them by stealing the most valuable thing they own."

"We could bring it back," Faye said.

"It would still be stealing," Indy said.

"It's the key to the Omega Book," Faye said. "It also may be our only chance of finding Kaspar."

"Too risky," Indy said.

"The famed scholar, adventurer, and grave robber concedes a challenge he can't meet?" Mystery asked mockingly.

"I prefer to rob my victims after they've been dead a few thousand years, not while they're still walking about," Indy said sourly. "We'll leave for Baghdad tomorrow, at first light. There is nothing more for us here."

Indy sat upright on the straw mat, awakened by the shouts of men and the ululation of the women in the center of the village. He glanced across the room and saw Faye sleeping, but not Mystery.

"Oh, no," he said.

"Where's Mystery?" Faye asked, rousing.

"I don't know," Indy said as he pulled on his shoes and grabbed his *zebun*. "But I'm afraid she may be the cause of all the excitement."

There was a crowd gathered around the temple, and everyone seemed to be talking at once in Arabic.

"What's wrong?" Indy asked Ali.

"The Staff is gone," Ali said. "We came here for morning worship, and it was missing. Where is it?"

"You can't think I stole it."

"I can think of no one else," Ali said. "I shouldn't have showed it to you. It was a mistake."

Ali made a motion with his hand, and Indy and Faye were grasped by their arms.

"Where is the girl?" Ali said.

"I don't know," Indy said.

"Again, where is the Staff?"

"Again, I don't know," Indy said.

Ali shook his head. He drew his *khanjer,* the blade of which gleamed in the pinkish light of dawn, and held it beneath Indy's chin.

"You will tell me," Ali said. "Better you tell me now than later, but you will tell me. Because I will start by peeling the skin from your arms and legs," he said. "The palms and the soles of the feet are particularly sensitive. Then, I will do the same to your chest and belly, and finally I will peel your face and scalp away. After that, when we recover the Staff, we will cut off your hands—"

"I know the rest," Indy said.

"Stake them down," Ali commanded.

The crowd grabbed Indy and Faye by their hands

and feet, then staked them spread-eagle on the sand with leather rope and wooden pegs.

"Do you have any ideas?" Faye asked.

"Not one," Indy admitted.

Ali sat cross-legged on the ground and removed Indy's left boot. Then he pulled the sock off and pressed the blade of the knife to the thin skin over the bone.

"We are a peaceful people," he said.

"Hitler says the same thing," Indy said.

"Who is this Hitler?"

"Guess," Indy said.

"You force us to do this," he said. Then Ali leaned close to Indy and said: "For fear of Shaitan, please tell us where you have hidden the Staff. I thought you were my friend. I do not want to hurt you. We will have to kill you now, of course, but I do not want to torture you."

"Then don't," Indy said.

Ali shook his head and began to trim the flesh from Indy's ankle. Indy gritted his teeth, but could not suppress a scream when he felt the blade of the knife skim along the bone.

"Stop!" Mystery shouted.

She emerged from the well, holding the Staff. Her hair was matted and she was covered with mud.

"I stole your stupid stick," she said. "I lowered

myself down the well and swam the underground spring to the chamber. Let them go."

Ali shouted in Arabic for the men to grab her.

"You touch me and I'll break this thing," Mystery said. "You let Indy and my mother go, and then I'll *think* about giving this back."

Ali told them to stop.

"We cannot release them," he told her. "It is our law."

"Then you can just say good-bye to your most precious possession," Mystery said and applied pressure to the Staff. It bent over her knee like a bow, and when it began to crack Ali held up his hand.

"All right," he said and told the others to cut Faye Maskelyne free.

"What about Dr. Jones?" Mystery asked.

"He abused my trust and my friendship," Ali said. "For that alone, he must die—as you must die, for stealing the Staff. But I will let your mother go."

Faye stood up, rubbing her wrists. She walked over and took the Staff from Mystery. A sudden cool wind rustled the coarse robes of the men and the scarves of the women, and Ali thought he saw something like the glow of phosphorus playing about the length of the Staff.

"Give me the Staff," Ali said. "Then go."

"I'm not leaving without my daughter," Faye said, her blue eyes flashing. "Or my friend."

"They are to die," Ali insisted. "Go."

"*Damn you*," Faye said and pointed the Staff at Ali. "You're not going to kill anybody."

A thin bolt of lightning descended from the cloudless sky and struck the sand at Ali's feet, knocking the *khanjer* out of his hand and sending him flying backward.

The crowd retreated.

"Wowser," Mystery said. "Do it again, Mom."

"I don't know what happened," Faye said as she walked over to Indy. She drew a knife from her belt and cut him loose. "I was just angry, that's all."

"Remind me not to make you angry," Indy said.

Ali sat up and shook his head. His turban and robe were smoking, and puddled on the ground was a red-hot fulgurite where the sand had melted together.

"Could it be?" he asked. "A woman?"

"What's he talking about?" Faye asked as she helped Indy to his feet. "How's your ankle?"

Indy wiggled his toes.

"Funny," he said, examining the wound. "It's just a scratch. I could have sworn that Ali carved a hunk out of my ankle like it was a Thanksgiving turkey. But it's not bleeding now, and it doesn't even hurt."

"May I examine the Staff?" Ali asked.

"Why should I give it back?" Faye asked.

"Please," Ali said. "Allow me to see it, if only for a moment."

He held out his hands pleadingly.

"Give it to him," Indy said as he put on his sock and boot.

Ali took the Staff and tested its weight.

"It is much heavier," he said. "Bring me a lamp."

Someone brought a lighted oil lamp, and he examined the length of the Staff with it. He ran his thumb over the letters.

"Look," he said. "They are quite clear now."

"What?" Faye asked.

"The Hebrew letters," Ali said, offering her the Staff back.

"The name of Aaron," Indy said.

"This is really it."

"Of course, Mom," Mystery said. "You think you can summon lightning with any old stick?"

"You are the Expected One," Ali said.

"I'm no such thing," Faye said.

"The Age of Miracles has returned," Ali said.

"I wouldn't argue with him," Indy whispered in her ear. "Grab the Staff and let's get out of here."

"A woman!" Ali said in amazement.

"I told you I wasn't it," Indy said.

"Ah, but that is the way with dreams," Ali said. "And our lives are but dreams while Allah sleeps and Shaitan plays. Our prayers are merely supplications to Allah to continue sleeping, for when he awakes—the world vanishes."

8

SNAKE CHARMERS

Two weeks later, in the Muski—the ancient section of Cairo—Indy braked the Indian to a stop in front of a tenement building that he had visited many times. Mystery, driving the Scout with Faye in the sidecar, pulled up behind him. Both motorcycles were covered in dirt and mud, and badly in need of repair.

"Wait here," he told the Maskelynes as he pulled the goggles from his dirty face. He walked up the flight of stairs to an apartment on the top floor of the building, wiped most of the dirt from his face with his kerchief, and knocked.

A dark-haired girl of about three came to the door.

"Is your daddy home?" Indy asked in Arabic.

She looked at him blankly.

Another child came to the door, a boy, a little older and bigger than the first child. Indy repeated the question. The boy nodded gravely, but did nothing further. Finally, another girl joined the two youngsters already at the door, and when Indy repeated the question yet one more time, she called into the house.

Indy could hear heavy footsteps pad across the wooden floor, and soon a familiar face appeared in the doorway.

"Sallah," Indy said. "It's me."

Sallah stared for a moment, as if he were looking at a ghost, and then broke into a wide grin.

"Let him in, my little ones," Sallah said. "This is our friend, Indiana Jones, who has come to pay us an unexpected visit. Come in, please."

"I have a couple of friends downstairs—"

"Invite them up as well," Sallah said. "No, wait, I will send one of the children to fetch them. Are you hungry? We can make something; it will be no trouble. You look as if you have come a great distance."

Sallah led Indy out onto the balcony, poured him some tea, and allowed him the most comfortable seat. The balcony overlooked a narrow alley, but beyond Indy could see the minarets and rooftops of Cairo.

"Forgive me for asking, my friend, but what spell

has some wizard put you under?" Sallah asked, concerned. "You don't look like yourself—a pale, tired, older imitation of yourself, perhaps."

Indy smiled.

"If I believed in the religion of my ancestors," Sallah continued, "I would have to conclude that your *ka* has come to visit me on its way to the underworld."

"I'm no ghost," Indy said. "I'll tell you the story sometime, but not now. Rest assured that it is really me. I'm surprised to catch you at home this time of day."

"The Depression is felt the world over," Sallah said. "There have been few digs in this area since the late twenties. In addition, the *Service des Antiquités* has been making it increasingly difficult to obtain permits to continue excavations at the more famous monuments."

"Hold that thought," Indy said as Faye and Mystery joined them.

Sallah stood and kissed both of their hands. In her left hand, Faye held the Staff, wrapped in a thin blanket.

"You did not tell me you were traveling with such beautiful companions," Sallah said.

"Please," Faye said. "I'm sure I look frightful."

"What do you have there, my radiant one?"

"Open it," Indy said.

Sallah unwrapped the blanket. The Staff had grown thicker and heavier, and was now a rich brown color. Sallah ran his fingers over the Hebrew lettering.

"Surely this is a modern fake," he said.

"No," Indy said. "It's the real McCoy."

"How can you be sure?"

"We had a demonstration of its power."

"But this wood shows hardly any signs of aging at all."

"When I first saw it," Indy said, "it was nothing but a desiccated stick. Since then, it has changed into what you see now. And it is what has brought us to Cairo."

Indy spent the next hour telling Sallah about the adventures he and the Maskelynes had shared. When he finished, Sallah scratched his dark beard and took a sip of his cold tea.

"Do you know what my people call the Sphinx?" he asked. " 'The Father of Terror.' It was once thought to be an eternal god, old beyond humanity."

"Will you help us?" Indy asked.

"Of course," Sallah said. "Anything I have to give, it is yours. But it will not be easy. We must work at night, and be prepared for the possibility of discovery—or intrusion. Tell me, this Japanese villain whom you blinded, is he still following you?"

"Not since Calcutta."

"Well, at least that is something," Sallah said. "We shall begin two nights from now. The moon will then be full, and it will help us to see while we are digging."

"Antiquities," the shopkeeper hissed. He was a gaunt man with a hawklike nose and a gold front tooth, with a cheap tarbush perched on his scalp, and wearing a dirty gray robe. "Priceless relics of a lost civilization. May I show you a royal scarab, perhaps?"

"We are not interested in your poorly made fakes," Sokai said.

"Sir, everything in this shop is genuine," the merchant said, pretending injury.

Jadoo was behind Sokai, and the old magician surveyed the contents of the shop with a practiced eye. There were the usual pieces of *ostraca,* limestone flakes bearing hieroglyphic prayers, building notes, and graffiti which had been gathered at the Giza necropolis; poor copies of funerary statues, the originals of which were housed at the museum in downtown Cairo; and assorted pieces of imitation jewelry, including copies of the golden beetle scarabs that adorned the breastplates of pharaohs.

"Sir, everything in this shop is genuine," the

merchant repeated. "I have dug most of these items from the sand myself."

"In that case, you must have dropped them on your dirty floor," Jadoo said. "None of these items have seen the interior of a royal tomb."

"You injure my pride," the shopkeeper said. "Tell me what it is you seek, and I will help you find it."

"Something a bit more exotic," Jadoo said.

"I can take you downstairs. There, we have things which we cannot offer for sale to the general public. Forbidden things. Things which one can mix a potion in to help heal wounds, restore virility, prolong life."

"Ah, now we are getting somewhere," Sokai said. He shook a Lucky Strike out of the pack, put it to his mouth, and allowed the shopkeeper to light it.

"We have the best four-thousand-year-old mummies," the shopkeeper continued. "Fresh from the tombs, ground up, and ready to be used. The very best medicinal mummy anywhere. Or, you can take a full mummy home as a conversation piece."

"What is your name?"

"Ahkmed, sir. And yours?"

"My name is unimportant," Sokai said. "What matters is that I am looking for a trio of mummies of rather more recent vintage."

"Of course," Ahkmed purred. "What dynasty?"

"What time is it?" Sokai asked.

Ahkmed looked shocked.

"Are you suggesting murder?" he asked.

"Come now," Sokai said. "Do not feign revulsion with me. I know that the mummies you have for sale downstairs were walking and talking just months ago, that you steal bodies from graves, wrap them up, and leave them out in the desert until they are dry enough."

Not knowing what else to do, Ahkmed smiled.

"We have made inquiries," Jadoo said, "and those in a position to know say that you are the man to approach if you want to get things done quickly and quietly."

"Ah, but it will not come cheaply," Ahkmed said.

"Of course not," Sokai said. He withdrew his wallet from his coat pocket, extracted five ten-pound notes, and placed them on the dirty counter. "We are not talking piastres here. There will be another one hundred pounds for you when the job is done."

Ahkmed looked to see if anyone was watching, then scooped up the notes and placed them in the pocket of his robe.

"Tell me about the three," he said.

"They are in Cairo," Sokai said, "but I am not sure where. An American archaeologist, a woman friend of his who is a magician, and the woman's daughter. I want the man most of all."

"What is this man's name?"

"Indiana Jones."

Ahkmed laughed.

"Do you know him?"

"Everyone in the Muski knows Dr. Jones," he said. "It will not be difficult to find him, but his death will not be a popular thing. He is well-liked by the diggers. I must ask three hundred pounds for his death."

"Jones is not worth that," Sokai said. "I will give two hundred."

"Agreed," Ahkmed said. "Tell me, what is Jones seeking in Cairo? It will help if I know a weakness, if I can make them come to me, where I can work at my leisure, instead of murdering them in their beds."

"The Sphinx," Jadoo said, then looked at Sokai. "They are here for the Sphinx. That is all we can tell you."

"And, I want everything that they are carrying," Sokai said. "Every scrap of paper, every object, no matter how insignificant it may seem. Bring it all to this address." Sokai handed him a business card containing the address of an export company. "Do you understand?"

"Perfectly," Ahkmed said. "And after?"

"Deliver them to me, of course," Sokai said. "As mummies."

*   *   *

Mystery shuffled the deck of cards while Sallah's children crowded around. She fanned the cards, face-out, and asked the youngest of the girls to pick one. Four-year-old Jasmine smiled, but was reluctant to take a card.

"Go ahead," her ten-year-old brother, Moshti, told her in Arabic. "It is all right. Choose a card."

Jasmine reached out and selected the three of clubs.

"Now, show it to your brothers and sisters," Mystery said. "I'm going to close my eyes so I don't see it. Don't anyone say the name, either."

Moshti translated, and Jasmine giggled as she waved the card around.

"Done?" Mystery asked, her eyes still tightly closed.

"Yes," Moshti said.

"All right, I want you to put the card back into the deck, anywhere at random," Mystery said, holding the closed deck in front of her. "Slip it in anywhere."

Moshti guided Jasmine's hand to the deck, where the card was inserted in approximately the middle.

"Done," Moshti said.

Mystery opened her eyes.

"Now, I'm going to try to find your card," she

told Jasmine. "Be very quiet, because this takes a great deal of concentration."

"What's concentration?" Moshti asked.

"Thinking," Mystery said as she took the first five cards from the deck and held them in her hand. "No, I don't think any of these are it," she said and let the cards fall. Then she took ten more cards from the top, but none of these met with her approval, either.

"Are you sure it's in here?" Mystery asked.

Moshti translated, and the children nodded.

"Okay," Mystery said and went through another twenty cards. "None of these are it, either. I'm just not finding it," she said, then dropped the rest of the deck onto the floor and held her hands palms-up.

"It has to be in there," Moshti said, and he and the children searched through the cards on the floor, but to no avail.

"Oh, wait a minute," Mystery said and thumped herself on the forehead. "That was my special flying card deck. How silly of me. I know where that card is."

She reached over and pulled the three of clubs from the back of Jasmine's dress.

"It flew over there," Mystery said.

The children applauded in delight.

"That was very good," Sallah said from across the room.

"It was one of the first tricks my father taught me," Mystery said as she gathered up the cards and returned them to the deck. "It's really a simple sleight-of-hand trick, but it always has been a crowd pleaser."

"I'm sure your father is very proud of you," Sallah said.

"How could he be when he hasn't seen me in years?" she asked angrily. "My mother and I apparently don't mean very much to him."

"Sometimes," Sallah said slowly, "parents must leave their children for a time because of the demands of our stomachs or of our dreams. I have been away from this brood for months at a time, at one dig or another. It doesn't mean I love them any less."

"You always come back," Mystery said.

"When parents don't," Sallah said, "it is often because of circumstances beyond their control. Your father loved you very much to teach you these tricks, and I'm sure that he wouldn't be away from you for any length of time by choice."

"Sometimes I think he's dead," Mystery said. "And sometimes I wish he was. The not knowing is the hardest part. I mean, if only my mother and I had a card, or a letter, explaining that he loved us but couldn't come back yet. That would mean so much."

"Of course it would," Sallah said. "None of us are young enough to be orphans. When I lost my own father I thought the world would come to an end, but it didn't. And my father lives on in the shining faces of these children you see before you."

"I'm never having kids," Mystery said. "The world is too hard. It would be cruel to bring another life into it."

"I said that when I was your age as well," Sallah said. "I hated the idea of children, of the responsibility of a family. But the world has an agenda of its own. And the peculiar thing about children, if they are loved and cared for and respected as human beings, is that they make the world a softer place."

Mystery made a face.

"You will see," Sallah predicted. "You will find the right young man and—"

"I've never had a boyfriend, you know," Mystery said. "My life has been so crazy. Tramping about the world, looking for my father, dressed half the time in men's clothing, hardly having finished a performance in one town before moving on to the next. Sometimes I wonder what it is like to have regular friends at all, much less a boyfriend."

"You have friends," Sallah said. "Indy is your friend. I am your friend, and your mother is certainly your friend."

"I want somebody who isn't old."

Sallah made a disapproving sound deep in his throat.

"You know what I mean," Mystery said.

"Yes," Sallah said, "and that is precisely what bothers me."

Mystery rolled her eyes.

"Perhaps a change of pace is needed," Sallah said. "Let me summon your mother and Indy. They will take you to the marketplace, where a new dress awaits."

"You mean a *real* dress?" Mystery asked. "With a skirt and everything?"

"Yes, with a skirt and everything," Sallah said.

"I can't believe I'm excited about this," Mystery said. "It's so . . ."

"Normal?" Sallah asked.

Mystery twirled in the middle of the street, and the white dress billowed out like a parachute around her, with the afternoon sun behind. An old Egyptian digging a trench at the curb paused long enough on the handle of his shovel to give a disapproving scowl, while a young man on a bicycle craned his neck and gave an appreciative whistle before colliding with the grille of a parked taxi.

"It's official," Indy said as the expected argument

ensued between the taxi driver and the bicyclist. "She's stopped traffic."

"I hadn't realized how much she had grown up," Faye said. "I didn't have curves like that when I was seventeen. How can she?"

"Better nutrition, maybe," Indy said. "Besides, you're so used to seeing her in men's clothing that anything else is bound to be a shock."

Street merchants called to them from the curbs, anxious to attract the attention of the wealthy Americans. Most of them wanted to read the fortunes in their hands or in tea leaves in exchange for a few piastres, or to scribble some mystical numbers on a slip of paper that would then be burned and consequently bring good fortune. Others held near-worthless trinkets in their outstretched hands, beads and costume jewelry mostly, while still others called in less strident voices offering things that were illegal even in the Muski: stolen goods, hashish, a few moments of passion with a stranger.

Mystery paused in front of a snake charmer.

The man was sitting cross-legged, playing a flute, in front of a wicker basket. A king cobra stuck its head out of the basket, inflated its hood, and seemed to sway in time to the strangely dissonant music.

"That's a big one," Faye said. "It must measure eight feet, tip to tail."

"How would you like for that monster to sink its fangs into you?" Mystery asked.

"Let's go," Indy said.

"The snakes are deaf, you know," Faye said. "They can't hear the music. They're responding to the movement of the flute, not the music."

"You must have seen this a thousand times already," Indy said.

"Yes, but this is one of the biggest snakes I've seen," Mystery said as she knelt down beside the snake charmer and gazed in the cobra's eyes. "Snake charming is a very old profession. Fathers pass it to their sons, and sometimes it's the only thing that puts food on a family's table."

Indy walked ahead a few paces.

"Very good," Mystery said as she laid a few coins on the ground. The snake charmer stopped the music and grinned broadly.

"I show you famous rope trick," he offered.

"Some other time," Mystery said.

Then, before she could say no, he grasped her hand and looked intently at her palm.

"You will live a long and eventful life," he said. "You will marry young, have many beautiful children, and your joy will always be greater than your sorrow."

"Promise?" Mystery asked.

"Dr. Jones," Faye chided. "I would never have guessed you were afraid of snakes."

"What are you talking about?" Indy asked with a wry smile. "It's that damn music I don't like."

A dark man in a red turban, who had been sitting on his heels with his face resting on his arms, suddenly looked up. He struck his walking stick three times against the pavement, and when Indy looked his way he asked softly, "Who would know the secret of the Sphinx?"

Indy stopped.

"What did you say?" he asked.

The man was silent.

Indy walked over, knelt on one knee, and peered at the man. The man returned his stare, but the leathery face revealed no hint of emotion.

"Dare to know the mysteries of the Sphinx?" the man asked.

"Come on," Faye said, tugging at Indy's shirt.

"Wait," Indy said.

"He's just a fortune-teller," Faye said.

"But he said something about the Sphinx," Indy said. "What do you mean, do I dare to know? Why do you ask me?"

"Your shadow walks with you," the man said. "You seek the Sphinx, and what it contains. I can help you."

"How?" Indy asked. "How can you help me?"

"Let's go," Faye said. "I don't like this."

"There is a map," Ahkmed said. "Very old. It shows many great mysteries surrounding the monument, mysteries that have yet to be revealed."

"Let me see it," Indy said.

"I do not have it," Ahkmed said. "But I can show it to you."

Indy hesitated.

"It is not far," Ahkmed said.

Faye crossed her arms.

"How much?" she asked.

"Not much," Ahkmed said.

"Take me there," Indy said. "We'll discuss how much it is worth after I've seen it."

Ahkmed nodded. He stood and led the trio through the winding streets to an alley, then down the alley to the back door of his shop. He knocked on the door, and it was opened by an unseen hand. They entered and Ahkmed beckoned them to follow him down a flight of stairs.

"I don't like this," Faye said.

"What can it hurt?" Indy asked. "He's probably got some useless piece of trash that's been reprinted a hundred times before. But, then again, he may have something that we really need. We've got to find out."

Indy went first, followed by Mystery and then Faye. The stairs creaked ominously with their weight, and the basement was so dark they could hardly see their feet.

"What's that smell?" Mystery asked. "I've never smelled anything so bad."

"Do you mind?" Indy asked as he reached the bottom of the steps. "Could we have some light here?"

Ahkmed struck a match and touched it to the wick of a kerosene lantern hanging from the ceiling. When he turned back around to face them, he held a rusty .32-caliber revolver tightly in his left hand. They heard the scratch of a key as the door above them was locked.

"A robbery?" Indy asked.

"I know where that smell is coming from," Mystery said.

An arm and a leg floated in a large vat of greenish liquid along the opposite wall, while on a wooden table beside it was a salt-encrusted corpse. The organs had been removed and lay in metal pails on the floor. On the bench was a bloody pair of long needle-nose pliers, with bits of brain still clinging to the jaws, and a big roll of wide linen bandages.

"You're making your own mummies," Indy said.

"Best in Cairo," Ahkmed said.

"Oh, my God," Faye said. "What have you got us into this time, Jones? I told you this was nonsense."

"Can we argue about this later?" Indy asked. "I've got a situation on my hands."

"We're involved in this, too," Faye shot back. "Or don't you think—"

"Silence!" Ahkmed shouted.

He waved the barrel of the gun.

"Come here, slowly."

They walked to the middle of the basement, beneath the lantern. Ahkmed approached Indy cautiously, gun at the ready, and snatched his revolver from the holster.

Ahkmed looked at the larger and well-oiled Webley for a moment, then threw his own gun onto the wooden bench. It struck one of the small baskets stacked there, and from inside there came the familiar furtive sounds of a snake looking for a way out.

"Your gun is much better," Ahkmed said admiringly.

"That was bright," Faye said. "I'll bet it's loaded, too."

"Don't start on me," Indy warned.

Ahkmed called out for someone named Abdul, and then they heard the basement door unlock above them. A seven-foot-tall Arab with a shaved head and glistening muscles walked down the protesting stairs. He was carrying a large wicker basket, which he placed in front of them.

"Take off your clothes," Abdul said. "Put them in the basket. Also, shoes, belts, billfold, everything."

"You've got to be kidding," Mystery said.

"Not kidding," Ahkmed said and cocked the revolver. "Take off your clothes, or I will have Abdul take them off for you."

Mystery looked over at Abdul, who was smiling in anticipation.

"What's going to happen after we do?"

Ahkmed made a motion with the barrel of the gun, and Abdul reached for Mystery. Indy stepped between them and placed a hand on Abdul's sweaty chest. It felt like pressing against a canvas bag full of steel ball bearings.

"Why don't you shoot me?" Indy asked Ahkmed.

"I will," Ahkmed threatened.

"No you won't," Indy said. "Because you don't want to puncture my hide, do you? It's hard to explain a bullet hole in a four-thousand-year-old mummy."

"It is strange, is it not, Dr. Jones?" Ahkmed asked. "Don't look so surprised—you are better known here than you have thought. And you are to become the very thing which you have sought for so many years."

"Well, I've got news for you, buddy. We all become history, one way or another, but I'm not going to speed up the process by climbing into that vat."

"Oh, yes you are," Ahkmed said. "Even if my cousin Abdul has to throw you into it."

Abdul grabbed Indy by the belt and collar and lifted him up. Facing the ceiling, the best Indy could do was to elbow Abdul in the head, and although the giant grunted at each blow, he did not ease his grip.

"No," Ahkmed said. "We must have his clothes and the contents of his pockets first."

Abdul put Indy down.

"Take off your clothes," Ahkmed said. "All of you. Do it!"

Indy slowly began to unbutton his shirt, beginning at the top. Faye and Mystery started to loosen their clothes as well, also slowly.

"Where's the Staff when you need it?" Indy asked Faye.

"Shut up," Faye said.

"What?" Ahkmed asked.

"Nothing," Indy said.

"You mentioned a staff."

"Maybe I did," Indy said.

"Is this staff valuable?"

"Priceless," Indy said. "But it's not important now, is it?"

He finished unbuttoning his shirt. Faye knelt down to undo the laces of her boots, while Mystery slipped the new dress from her shoulders.

"Tell me about it," Ahkmed said.

"It would take too long," Indy said as he pulled out his shirttails. "And you're obviously in a hurry to get us in that brine solution."

The barrel of the gun wavered.

Both Ahkmed and Abdul were staring at Mystery in her underwear, their eyes bright with anticipation.

Reaching behind his back and pretending to free his shirttail, Indy grabbed the whip instead and came forward with it. The whip cracked as it bit into Ahkmed's wrist, and the gun went off just before Ahkmed dropped it and staggered backward into the wooden bench. The bullet struck the masonry wall behind him. The wooden bench toppled over, spilling the corpse and the baskets of snakes onto the floor.

Cobras darted in every direction.

"Snakes!" Indy yelled. "Lots and lots of snakes!"

Abdul seized Indy by the back of the neck with a hamlike fist and began to drag him toward the vat. A nine-foot cobra slithered up his leg and Abdul tried to shake it off.

The cobra hissed and opened its hood, then sank its fangs into Abdul's thigh. The giant yelped and grasped the snake with both hands, but could not pull it free. When he turned to plead for Indy to remove it, Indy drew back and hit him on the chin with his best punch.

Abdul staggered backward and fell face-forward into the vat. The liquid sizzled and hissed.

Ahkmed was already dead. Several snakes hung from his face, and there were many red and puckered bite marks across his cheeks.

"Let's get out of here," Indy said.

He jumped onto the stairs.

"Don't you want your gun?" Mystery asked as she slipped the straps of the dress back on.

"Forget it," Indy said, coiling the whip and hanging it at his belt.

Mystery shook her head, then walked calmly across the floor.

"Don't!" Indy said.

"Shhh," Faye said. "Don't interrupt her concentration."

Mystery continued forward, stepping over the writhing snakes, and picked up the Webley.

"They're just trying to find a way out," Mystery said. "Ahkmed was a goner, but Abdul probably would have survived if he hadn't panicked. A cobra bite is not normally lethal."

"I'll take your word for it," Indy said as he slipped the Webley into its holster.

"What do they do with the—*things* they make?" Mystery asked.

"There's quite a black market for powdered mummy," Indy said. "Some people use it as a medicine, while others believe it's a powerful aphrodisiac."

"How revolting," Mystery said. "Shouldn't we burn this place or something?"

"We would, if it wasn't attached to honest shops and homes on either side," Indy said. "We'll just have to leave it for the snakes to take care of."

9

JACKALS

They drove to the Giza plateau shortly before sunset in a rickety old Ford owned by Sallah's brother-in-law, parked the car near the Nile beneath a sand-bank so as not to attract attention, and waited for the moon to rise. When it did, rising like some ghostly messenger over Cairo two hours later, a jackal howled in the distance. The howl drove the last of the tourists back across the bridge to the safety of Cairo, leaving the monuments to the desert and the things that lived there.

Sallah picked up the canvas bag of torches soaked in pine tar and the heavy iron pry bar, and Indy got the shovels and axes. Faye carried the Staff and a pair of lanterns, while Mystery carried the ropes and tackle.

They climbed up the rocky bank of the Nile and made their way across the tortured landscape toward the Sphinx. As they grew closer, the Sphinx's head emerged from the horizon, along with the peaks of two of the three pyramids beyond. Finally, they threaded their way around the toppled columns and stones of the temple to arrive at the mouth of the enclosure itself.

Before them was the enigmatic face of the Sphinx, staring perpetually to the east. The ragged paws jutted toward them, while the head, with its protruding ears and ribbed hood, seemed ready to topple forward onto them at any moment, so badly damaged was it. Because the Sphinx was carved from a single limestone outcropping, the head was the only thing that appeared above the horizon; the rest of the body was set into a trenchlike enclosure.

Between the paws was an upright granite monument, about the height of a person, that was covered with hieroglyphics. Like the Sphinx itself, the monument was damaged and incomplete.

"There's something about this place," Faye said. "You can feel the ages pressing down upon you. No, not just the ages, but all of eternity."

"You're not the first person to note that," Indy said. "I felt it too, the first time I came here as a boy. Much more of the Sphinx is exposed now than it was. Its history has been one of alternately being buried by the desert and being dug out by later generations."

"Won't anybody notice that we're snooping around here?"

"It's not likely," Indy said. "We're so well-hidden by the enclosure that they would have to be right on top of us before they discovered us."

"What does this say?" Mystery asked, standing in front of the granite stelae. The moon was so bright that Indy could read it without the aid of a lantern.

"It's like most government monuments," he said. "It commemorates a public works project and the leader who instituted it. About twenty-five centuries ago, Thutmose IV cleared out the sand around the Sphinx and made repairs to it. Because we have part of a name down here on the damaged portion of the tablet, the single syllable 'Khaf,' most Egyptologists believe the Sphinx was built a thousand years earlier, by Khafre."

"What do you think?" Mystery asked.

"I think we don't have all the answers yet," he said.

"I've read that Napoleon used the Sphinx for target practice," Mystery said, "and shot off the nose."

"No, it was disfigured by an Islamic zealot in the fourteenth century," Indy said.

"All right, Indy," Sallah said as he set down his

bundle and picked up a shovel. "I am ready. Where do we start?"

"Good question," Indy said. "Faye, it's time."

Faye nodded.

She walked to the Sphinx, then turned and sat between the paws, with the Staff across her lap. She lowered her head and concentrated, remaining this way for a quarter of an hour while the others waited in silence.

Finally her head came up.

Faye opened her eyes, but she looked as if she were listening to distant music. She placed one foot beneath her and then the other, and finally she held the Staff out in front of her at arm's length.

She walked forward seven paces, hesitated, and took a step to the left. She held the Staff over her head with one hand, then twirled it as she brought it down. The end of the Staff sank into the shallow sand and struck something hard beneath.

"Dig here," she said.

"Are you sure?" Indy asked. "There wasn't any lightning or anything. I expected more."

"When the Israelites looked for water in the desert," Faye said, "they simply struck a rock with the Staff, and a spring flowed. Why should this be any different?"

"Well, thousands—no, probably millions—of people have crossed that particular spot over the last five thousand years, and nobody's found anything there. It sounded like the Staff struck the natural limestone beneath the sand."

"Quit complaining and dig," Faye said.

Sallah marked the spot with his foot, then started to clear away the sand with a shovel. Indy and Mystery moved to help while Faye watched, the Staff held upright in her hand. In a few minutes they had enough sand removed to see a smooth, flat surface.

"It's man-made," Indy said. "But it could just be one of the flagstones of the old courtyard here."

"Keep digging," Faye said.

Sallah tapped the stone with the blunt end of the pry bar. There was a hollow ring.

"I'll be damned," Indy said.

Sallah looked up disapprovingly.

"I found an edge," Mystery said.

Within half an hour they had removed all of the dirt from the stone, which was flat and about a yard square. Then Sallah drove the pry bar beneath one edge of it.

"Not yet," Indy said. "Mystery, make sure the coast is clear."

Mystery nodded.

"Be careful," Indy added.

She scrambled up the right paw, climbed onto the shoulder of the Sphinx, and leaned against the head. The moon was high in the sky now.

Mystery looked behind her. The body of the Sphinx, nearly the length of a football field, looked out of proportion; the head seemed too small for such a huge body. Jutting into the sky in the north-east, and well-illuminated by the moon, was the Great Pyramid of Khufu, the last remaining wonder of the Ancient World. Nearly directly behind the Sphinx was the somewhat lesser Pyramid of Khafre, while to the southwest was the smallest of the three great pyramids on the Giza plateau, that of Menkure.

She thought she saw something move to the south, parallel to the Nile. She closed her eyes, then looked again, but there was nothing.

"All clear," Mystery shouted.

As she came back down, a piece of the Sphinx from a thousand-year-old patch sloughed away beneath her feet. She caught herself before she fell more than a few feet.

"I told you to be careful," Indy said.

"Sorry."

"Don't be sorry next time," Indy said. "Be safe."

Sallah took a deep breath, gritted his teeth, and leaned on the end of the bar.

Nothing happened.

He took a better grip on the bar and put his back into it. The muscles in his arms and shoulders bulged like snakes, but again nothing moved.

"It can't be that heavy," Indy said.

"Would you like to try?" Sallah asked. His face was red and his nose dripped sweat.

"You must not have good leverage," Indy said.

"How long do you think I've been doing this?"

"Let me try," Indy said. "That stone can't weigh more than a couple of hundred pounds."

He spit on his hands, repositioned the bar, and tugged.

"You're right," Indy said.

"Let's try it together," Sallah said.

Sallah took the top of the bar while Indy took the middle and Mystery pushed from the other side. After thirty long seconds of concerted effort, there was the sound of rock scraping against rock.

"It's moving," Indy said through clenched teeth.

"Keep going," Sallah urged.

Reluctantly, the stone yielded.

Mystery relinquished her grip on the bar and stepped back. She wiped the sweat from her brow with the back of her hand, and then looked up at the stars.

"It's funny," she said, her chest heaving. "I thought I would be excited at this moment, but I'm not. I feel strange—like I'm one of the jackals we hear out there on the desert."

"We are jackals," Sallah said, his eyes shining. "It is not a bad thing, it is the order of nature. My family has been scavenging these tombs for generations. We are simply human jackals. *Raiders*."

10

FATHER OF TERROR

Sallah wrestled the large stone to one side while a gust of hot air issued from the passage, causing the Sphinx and the stars above to shimmer like a mirage.

"Take a deep breath, Indy," Sallah said. "We breathe the air of pharaohs!"

"And slaves," Indy said as he took a torch from the canvas sack slung over his shoulder. He struck a wooden match on the limestone block that Sallah eased onto the sand, then touched it to the tightly wrapped bundle of pitch-laden reeds. The torch sputtered before bursting into a steady orange flame.

Indy took a few steps into the passage and held the torch in front of him. The stairs were covered with a fine red dust, and led down into darkness.

The walls of the passage were plain, but there were hieroglyphics on the lintel.

"The hieroglyphs," Sallah said. "What do they say?"

"They urge the wise to proceed and the foolish to turn back," Indy said.

"You never took advice before," Sallah said.

"You're very funny," Indy said. "You're also coming with me."

"But Indy," Sallah stammered. "Who will protect the women?"

"You want to stay up here with Faye and that stick?"

Sallah looked uncertain, then hurried to join Indy.

"I hope I have made the right choice," he said.

"We'll know soon enough," Indy said as he handed him a torch. "Stay behind me. Don't touch anything unless I tell you to."

The steps descended sharply into the earth, then leveled out into a narrow room decorated with colorful and elaborate paintings. The goddess Nut, with lines of stars running down her sides, spanned the ceiling. On the walls were reliefs depicting priests preparing a pharaoh for his journey to the underworld. The ankh, the Egyptian symbol of eternal life, was repeated again and again. Two clay vases filled with rolls of papyrus were on either side of the entrance to the room.

"This is the second passage," Indy said. "So far, the chamber is following a rather standard layout, common to most royal tombs."

Indy picked up a papyrus roll and carefully unfolded it a few inches. It was written in a cursive form of hieroglyphics known as hieratic.

"Do you have any idea how old this labyrinth is?" Sallah asked.

"No," Indy said. The edges of the papyrus he held began to crumble to dust. He replaced it in the vase and picked out another one, which also began to crumble when he unrolled it. "These are testimonials of the priests who apparently restored the chamber at intervals of several hundred years. This one dates back to the time of Rameses II, thirteen hundred years before the birth of Christ. It says this spot is old beyond reckoning, and is the place of the glorious First Time."

"The First Time," Sallah said. "The time when the gods came to earth. I thought it was just a fable. Now, here, it seems more real than life itself. What do you think, my friend?"

"I think this isn't the time to debate theology," Indy said. "The ancient Egyptians had a much different view of reality than we do. They took it as fact that their pharaohs were direct descendants of the gods."

Indy replaced the papyrus and brushed the dust from his palms.

"I'm not going to look at any of the others for fear of destroying irreplaceable texts," he said. The weight of ages seemed to be pressing down upon him.

"If only there were time," Sallah said.

"But there's not," Indy said. "Ironic, isn't it?"

"I hate irony," Sallah said. "It usually leads to trouble."

"Come on," Indy said. "We're safe enough in this chamber, I think. It will be this next one where things start to get a little dicey."

"I hate dicey," Sallah said.

Indy stopped at the top of another series of steps. He thrust the torch into the darkness. On either side of the steps, in alcoves cut into the limestone walls, shone golden statues about half the size of a human being.

"The third passage," Indy said. "And the sanctuaries in which the gods of the east and west repose. Let me go first."

"If you insist," Sallah said.

Indy took a cautious step down, and then another.

"So far, so good," Indy said over his shoulder.

"When you follow, step in the prints left by my boots in the dust."

Indy took another step.

On the left, the gods of the east gleamed in their alcoves, and they were matched on the right by the gods of the west. They were all fierce-looking monsters, many of them half human and half animal, each of them with a part to play in the ancient Egyptian pantheon: Horus, the avenger, with a falcon's head; Anubis, god of the underworld, with the head of a jackal; Ammon, the patron of the pharaohs, with a ram's head; Hathor, the goddess of childbirth, with the head of a cow.

Indy felt the tread he was standing on sink a fraction of an inch.

"Oh, no," he said.

The golden jaw of the jackal-headed figure of Anubis dropped open, revealing rows of gleaming ivory teeth. Indy rolled forward as a copper-tipped dart shot from its throat and embedded itself in the limestone wall.

As Indy rolled down the remaining steps, a fusillade of darts followed, a fraction of a second too late to hit their mark. Indy was expecting the pit at the bottom of the steps, and by the time he reached it, the whip was out and its tip was wrapping around the cornice of a stone column in the next room.

Indy dropped the torch and swung with both hands from the handle of the whip. He watched as the torch landed in the sand twenty feet below, sending dozens of scorpions scurrying away from it.

Then the stone column, dislodged by Indy's weight, toppled over. It bridged the pit, but dropped Indy low enough that the toes of his boots were scraping the sand.

His hat fell into the pit.

"Indy, my friend!" Sallah called. "Are you all right?"

Indy retrieved his hat, then scurried hand-over-hand up the whip to the column.

"Yes," he called as he took another torch from the canvas bag and lit it with a match he struck on the column. "Come on, and be careful crossing."

Sallah walked carefully over the stone column to join Indy on the other side of the scorpion pit, then picked a scorpion off the crown of the fedora and threw it back into the pit.

"Thanks," Indy said.

"They won't kill you," Sallah said, "but for a day or so they make you wish they had. Where are we now?"

"The room of the two guardians," Indy said, then held the torch aloft. "Meet the guardians."

The desiccated corpse of a warrior was tucked into a niche in the east wall. His skin had shrunken against his bones, his armor was tarnished, but his spear was still tightly grasped in a skeletal hand.

On the opposite side was a priest. His white tunic had rotted away, and his head had fallen backward from his shoulders, while his jaw had dropped down to rest on his sternum. Yellowed teeth bristled from the gaping mouth. In his hand he held a copper adze.

"How do we proceed?" Sallah asked.

"Very carefully," Indy said.

Indy stepped forward, paused, then took another step forward.

"Anything?" he asked.

"Nothing," Sallah said.

"Good," Indy said, taking two more paces. "How about now?"

"Everything seems . . . too easy," Sallah said.

"You're right," Indy said.

The torch flickered, its flame kissed by the slightest of breezes.

"Get down!" Indy shouted.

Indy hugged the floor as a copper disk with razor-sharp edges dropped from the ceiling. The disk swung low enough to slice through the back of Indy's leather jacket, then swung up over Sallah's arched back and returned to the ceiling.

"You okay?" Indy asked as he picked up the torch.

"I think so," Sallah allowed.

"Good," Indy said. "The next chamber, the fifth, should be a well room."

With Sallah at his heels, Indy walked cautiously down the passage to the entrance of the next chamber. As predicted, there was a pit in the middle of it, surrounded by four massive, square pillars. The pillars were decorated with stylized depictions of crocodiles and baboons.

Indy sat on his heels for a moment while he studied the room. Then he took a pebble from the floor and tossed it into the pit.

A few feet down, it bounced sharply on stone.

"We walk across it," he said.

"Are you sure?"

"Don't touch the pillars or the floor," Indy said as he stepped down into the pit and walked across the flagstones to the other side.

"What will happen if I do?" Sallah asked.

"I don't know," Indy said, "but it won't be good."

Indy stepped up on the other side of the pit, then waited for Sallah to join him.

"In a typical tomb," Indy said, "the next chamber would be the burial chamber—unless the tomb was extended to a second course, in which case the chamber would become the 'Chariot Hall,' a sort of war memorial."

They stepped into the next room, which was a

large chamber decorated with scenes of warfare: phalanxes of soldiers, thundering chariots, rows of decapitated enemies. In the middle of the room, centered among the pillars, was a flat-topped stone monument with rows of ankhs on each side. Unlike the previous rooms, there was no obvious exit.

"There must be a second level," Sallah said.

"All we have to do is find the entrance without killing ourselves," Indy said.

"A worthy goal," Sallah said.

Indy searched the floor and the walls by the light of the torch. There was a confusing array of paintings and reliefs and, along the north wall, a series of oval cartouches containing the names of pharaohs.

"Look at this," Indy said.

"The names of every king to rule Egypt since Menes in the First Dynasty," Sallah said as he held his torch close. "And look, the names go all the way back to the Thirtieth Dynasty in the Late Period."

"That's impossible," Indy said incredulously. "This labyrinth could not have been built before the Middle Kingdom."

"Yet," Sallah said, "here are the names. Even I can read them."

"They must have been carved here during the restorations," Indy said.

"Let us hope so," Sallah replied. "The alternative is too frightening to contemplate."

Indy turned from the wall to examine the stone monument in the center of the room.

"Perhaps this is a burial chamber after all," Sallah suggested.

"This is too small to hold a mummy," Indy said.

"What if it holds the body of a child?" Sallah asked. "Or a temple animal, such as a baboon?"

"I don't think so," Indy said as he rapped it with his knuckles. "It sounds solid. Say, how far do you think we've gone?"

"Into the earth?" Sallah asked.

"No," Indy said. "Distance."

"It is hard to say," Sallah replied. "I was not counting the steps, but I would say it has been several hundred meters, at least."

"And in which direction?" Indy asked.

"Southwest," Sallah said.

"That's what I thought," Indy said as he jumped up on the flat surface of the stone monument. "We're underneath the Great Pyramid. We don't go down—we go up!"

Indy held the torch close to the ceiling and probed with the fingers of his other hand. Then he pushed with his palm, and the ceiling seemed to give upward.

"Help me," Indy said. "I think it's cantilevered."

Sallah clambered up the other side of stone monument and, holding the torch between his teeth, put both of his meaty palms against the ceiling and pushed.

With a creaking groan, the ceiling swung open as a fine layer of red dust sprinkled down. A narrow flight of steps led upward.

"Another first corridor," Indy said as he pulled himself into the atticlike space. Then he extended a hand down and helped Sallah struggle up into it.

"I've never seen anything like this," Sallah said, excitement showing in his eyes for the first time. "What did the ancients call it?"

"I don't know," Indy admitted. "This is a new one for me. But we have gone deep within the earth, and now we are starting our ascension—it must have religious connotations. Let's call it the Shaft of Redemption."

"What do you suppose we will find at the end?" Sallah asked. "Think of Carter's discovery of the tomb of Tutankhamen—and he was a minor king! Think what we might find here!"

"I'm afraid to," Indy said. "Be careful—these stairs are steep, and the dust makes them slippery as well."

After thirty steps, with no landing yet in sight, Sallah braced himself against a wall and wiped the sweat from his face with a kerchief.

"I'm sorry, my friend," he said. "My wind is failing me."

"No problem," Indy said, pausing. "I can use a rest myself. Let me know when you're ready to go on."

Sallah held a finger to his lips.

"Did you hear that?" he asked. "A rustling, almost as if someone were following us."

"These tombs sigh and moan like living things after they're opened," Indy said. "It's the change in atmospheric pressure, and the limestone drawing moisture from the air."

"This was something else," Sallah said. "Footsteps, I believe."

"Your ears are more sensitive than mine," Indy said.

"It is the Bedouin in me," Sallah said and smiled. "You go ahead. I am going to remain here for a few minutes, to make sure that we are not being followed."

"I'd feel better if—"

"Indy?"

There was a light at the bottom of stairs, and Mystery climbed lithely into the corridor. She was holding a battery-powered lantern, and she still had the coil of rope slung over her shoulder.

"Up here," Indy called. "Be careful."

When she had joined them, Indy told her: "Next time you go tomb-hopping, carry a torch with you.

The flame will tell you when you've hit a pocket of bad air."

"I don't plan on a next time," Mystery said.

"Is your mother all right?" Indy asked.

"She sent me to check on *you*," Mystery said. "It seems like you've been gone an awfully long time. But seeing the darts and the pits, I can understand why."

"You shouldn't have tried to negotiate them alone," Indy said in his best adult voice.

"I'm here, aren't I?" she asked.

"Well, you're just going to have to come along," Indy said. "I'm not sending you back by yourself."

"Go on," Sallah said. "I need my rest, and you need to work as quickly as possible. Dawn is not so far away. If there is trouble, I will shout out."

Indy clasped his old friend on the shoulder. Then he turned to Mystery. "Follow me," he said, "but do so carefully." With that, he resumed his ascent of the stairway.

Faye saw Jadoo's shadow, cast by the light of the full moon low in the sky, on the sand at her feet. She pushed the sleeves of her robe back to reveal her arms, brushed her dark hair away from her face, then turned to face the surprised magician.

"I knew you would come," she said. "But I have

to admit, I was expecting something a little more artful than your simply sneaking up behind me."

"Ah, but it is effective," Jadoo said, regaining his composure. "Particularly when I bring an armed company with violence in their hearts."

Sokai and Lieutenant Musashi dropped down into the Sphinx enclosure, followed by Warrant Officer Miyamoto and a half dozen Japanese soldiers armed with submachine guns. Miyamoto barked orders and the soldiers trained their guns on Faye.

Jadoo closed the distance between himself and Faye and snatched the Staff from her hands.

"I never dreamed it would be in such fine shape," he exclaimed. "It has such weight still, and the wood has such a wonderful texture, almost as if it were part of a living tree." He brought the Staff to within inches of his nose. "The smell of fresh almonds!"

Faye crossed her arms and regarded Jadoo with scorn. A gentle wind came from the east, sending old newspapers and other trash skittering across the sand while gently stroking Faye's hair. Jadoo did not remember her hair being so shot full of gray.

"Tell me, have you attempted to conjure with it?"

Faye was silent.

Jadoo held the Staff in front of him, unsure of

what to do next. Then he pointed it at the sky and commanded it to produce hail.

Faye laughed.

"No matter," Jadoo said. "I will find the words."

"I see that your little band of misfits has done much of the work for us," Sokai said as he approached. "I am particularly grateful that Dr. Jones has volunteered to test the passage for pitfalls. Tell me, are his fat friend and your tomboy daughter with him?"

Faye shrugged.

"So brave," Sokai commented with feigned sadness, "and yet so foolish."

"I have always listened to my heart instead of my head," she said.

Sokai parted his trench coat and drew his samurai sword from its folds. He leveled the sword at Faye, placed the tip right beneath her chin, and pushed just hard enough to draw a drop of blood.

"If you so much as call out," he said, "these soldiers will kill you. And if you cause trouble here on the surface while I am down there, I will without the slightest hesitation kill your brat. Do you understand?"

"Yes," Faye said.

"Good," Sokai said as he sheathed his sword. "Warrant Officer Miyamoto, keep a close watch on this American bitch. Lieutenant Musashi, follow me."

The stairs ended in a small room with no decoration. A small, square hole in the ceiling led to a long shaft.

"Give me a boost," Indy said.

Mystery put her hands together to make a stirrup for Indy's right boot, then helped lift him up to the ceiling. He put his hands on either side of the chimneylike shaft, but the pain from his injured shoulder made him wince and give a small cry.

"Let me," Mystery said.

"No, I can do it," Indy said as he dropped back down. "I just need a minute."

"We don't have a minute," Mystery said as she adjusted the coil of rope. "Let me, and then I can lower the rope for you. This is my type of thing, Dr. Jones."

"Too dangerous," he said.

"How dangerous do you think it will be when you fall twenty feet and land on this rock floor?" she asked as she jumped up and grasped the lip of the shaft, which only projected out a fraction of an inch, with her fingertips. She hung there for a moment, and then pulled herself up into the shaft, with her back to one wall and her feet against the other. She kicked off her shoes.

"All right," Indy said. "But be careful. Go slowly, and don't touch anything that looks suspicious. If you feel anything move, get out of the shaft quick."

"Don't you think I know anything?" Mystery asked.

"Yes, I do," Indy said. "I've just gotten kind of used to having you around, is all."

"I see a beam up above me," Mystery said as she made her way higher. She gave no sign that she recognized Indy's expression of fatherly sentiment.

"Is it wood or stone?" Indy asked.

"It's metal," she said.

"What kind?" Indy asked. "Copper?"

"Nope," Mystery said. "It's iron."

"It can't be iron," Indy said. "The structures at Giza were built before the Iron Age."

"Sure," she said. While Indy debated whether she should touch it, she grasped the beam and swung up into the next chamber. She tucked the lantern under one arm as she tied the rope around the beam. "It looks like iron, it feels like iron, it's as strong as iron, but it's not iron."

"Don't touch it," Indy called.

"Too late," Mystery said as she dropped the coil down the shaft.

Indy put his torch in his teeth, grasped the rope, and fought his way up the shaft to the beam to join Mystery. He found himself in a fairly spacious chamber of finished limestone, with no feature other than the beam—which Indy had to admit was iron—and a doorway to the north.

"Good job," Indy said.

"Thanks."

"The next chamber," Indy said and nodded toward the doorway. "The Hall of Truth. If the book truly exists, it will be in there. Are you ready?"

"I've been ready since I was twelve," Mystery said.

The entrance to the room was flanked by two massive marble columns; the one on the left was black, while the other was a brilliant white.

Indy held the torch aloft and stepped through the doorway, followed by Mystery and her electric lantern. There was a wavering musical chord, a major chord.

Mystery switched off her lantern.

It wasn't needed.

The room had become illuminated by some diffused, unseen light source. The floor, walls, and ceilings of the room were polished, rose-colored granite. In the middle of the room was a black granite pillar, and in relief on the pillar were a number of characters from various ancient languages— Sumerian, Egyptian, Sanskrit, Coptic, Greek, Chinese, and a couple that Indy did not recognize.

The only character that Mystery recognized was the Greek one.

On the pillar was a book, or something that resembled a book but wasn't quite like any book either of them had ever seen: The pages of the book were of a highly polished, silvery metal, and they rippled—in time to the wavering music set off by the disturbance of the air that Indy and Mystery had caused merely by entering the room. The pages turned upon a golden spine, but they also went down inside the pillar, so that the book appeared endless.

"The Omega Book," Mystery said.

"Now I know I'm dreaming," Indy said.

"Does this feel like a dream?" Mystery asked as she pinched his forearm.

"No," Indy said, rubbing the spot.

"Then quit talking nonsense," she said. "My father said the book existed, and he was right. But this looks more like a machine or something than a book."

"The Ancient of Days, perhaps?" Indy asked as he tossed the torch onto the bare rock floor of the room behind them.

"What?" Mystery asked.

"The divine . . . *something* that gave mercy and bread to the Israelites each morning," Indy said. "Some people have said that the Bible's description of it sounds a little like a Stone Age people attempting to describe an automobile—eyes for headlights, a mouth for the radiator, that sort of thing."

"What do you think?"

"This could be it, and I wouldn't know."

"I wonder where the light is coming from," she said.

"From recessed mirrors or polished plates or crystals in the walls or ceiling," Indy responded. "I've seen some barrows in England which achieved nearly the same effect with light from the mid-winter sun."

"Dr. Jones," Mystery said. "It's night outside, remember?"

"That is a problem with my theory," Indy said. "Anyway, be careful. There have been no traps or pitfalls so far to speak of on the second level, but there must be something deadly here."

"Maybe it's the book," Mystery said.

Indy nodded as he walked over to the pillar. He leaned down to examine the book, and the force of his breath turned the shimmering pages. On the right side, new pages rose to take the place of those that had disappeared into the base of the pillar.

"Are we on the wrong side?" Mystery asked. "Is the book upside down?"

"No," Indy said. "These ancient languages generally read from right to left."

He gently lifted a page between the thumb and index finger of his right hand. The page was so thin and light that he could not feel it between his fingers. The characters, which were about the size of newspaper type, were somehow cut into the page. There was a rainbow of colored sheets of the same material on top of the pillar.

"Can you read it?" Mystery asked.

"No," Indy said. "It doesn't make any sense to me. I wonder what these other sheets are for."

Mystery picked up the red sheet that was on top.

"This stuff is amazing," she said. "You bend it, and it springs right back into shape."

She experimented a moment with it, then crumpled it in a tight ball between her hands. When she released it, the sheet unfolded back into a perfect, uncreased page.

"I had this game when I was a child," she said. "It was a code book, and to read it you had to put a colored page over it. I wonder if it works like that."

Indy took the red sheet and slipped it behind the page.

"I'll be," he said. "Look, Chinese and Sanskrit and some other language I don't know."

Indy took the next sheet, which was blue, and slipped it behind the same page. Three columns of text appeared—one in Egyptian, one in Coptic, and the last in Greek.

"This is incredible," Indy said. "I've never seen anything like it—the *world* has never seen anything like it, at least not the world we know. We'll have to rewrite history. This is the archaeological discovery of the age."

"What's the page about?" Mystery asked.

"It's the life of a French farmer named François Malevil," Indy said. "Like the Rosetta stone, the three translations are identical. The dates are also given in different numbering systems. Let's see, it will take me a moment to reconcile the Greek with our present system."

Indy paused for a moment.

"The fourteenth century," he said. "*After Christ.* No, that can't be right. My God, it is. Look, this entry talks about a Roman soldier who died at Actium."

Indy gave in to his first instinct: He began turning the pages an inch at a time, scanning the names, eagerly searching for "Jones."

"This thing isn't in alphabetical order," he complained.

"What are you doing?" Mystery asked.

"Of course," Indy said, glancing at the dates. "It's in chronological order."

"What are you looking for?"

"My own name."

"No," Mystery said. "You can't. We aren't supposed to know."

"The book—," he stammered.

"Don't you see?" she said. "This is the last trap. You can look up anybody else's name but your own. You've got the ultimate archaeological reference here. Look up Jesus or Joan of Ark, but not Indiana Jones."

Indy stopped.

"I'm right," Mystery said. "You know I am."

"Seventeen-year-olds are so sure of themselves."

"This one certainly is," she said. "The world isn't ready for this."

"Then what are we doing here?" Indy asked.

"I'm here for one reason only, and that's to find out what happened to my father," Mystery said. "You're here because I can't read any of the languages that book is written in."

Indy paused.

"What's wrong?" she asked.

"I hadn't thought of that before," Indy said. "There are people missing from my life I'd like to look up, but I don't think I should."

He flipped through the book, looking for the 1930s.

"The book gets thicker as you go forward in time," he said. "More people to keep track of, I guess. Okay, I'm getting close. Going through the twenties now."

Mystery nodded.

"Let's see," Indy said. "Maskelyne . . . Believe it or not, there are several. When was your father born?"

"Eighteen ninety-three."

"Okay, Kaspar Maskelyne. Born July 16, 1893, at Leeds."

"That's him."

Indy ran his finger down the text, reading to himself.

"Yes?" Mystery asked.

"This stuff isn't as easy to read as the baseball scores in the morning paper," Indy said as he took a green sheet and inserted it behind the page. "I'm not all that fluent in Sanskrit, okay? Let me check it with—"

The wavering music chimed again.

"Dr. Jones," Sokai said as he stamped out Indy's smoldering torch in the outer room with the heel of an expensive but well-scuffed black shoe. "Don't you know you shouldn't be so careless with fire?"

Lieutenant Musashi, who was behind him, laughed wickedly.

Sokai unsheathed his sword as he entered the room.

"I see that you have found the prize which we all seek. Is it as exciting as we had hoped?"

"Where's Sallah?" Indy asked.

"We found him in the corridor," Sokai said. "He is now outside, with the woman, being guarded by Warrant Officer Miyamoto and his troops. Move away from the book."

Indy did so.

"How unfortunate for you that we meet again. I will be extracting more than an eye in restitution from you. I was thinking an organ closer to your . . . well, heart, for lack of a better word, would do nicely and we'd go on from there. Wouldn't want you to die too quickly now, would we?"

"Don't get your hopes up," Indy said.

"Who is this creep?" Mystery asked.

"This is Sokai," Indy said. "He's the one who started all this trouble for me in the first place."

"Quiet," Sokai said as he handed the sword to Musashi. "Skewer them if they move."

Sokai approached the book, his one good eye gleaming in the soft light. He leaned over to examine the page, then frowned.

"What's wrong?" Indy taunted. "Can't read Sanskrit?"

"Get over here," Sokai demanded, not realizing that another of the colored sheets would have rendered the text in Mandarin, a language he could read.

Indy walked over slowly.

"How does this work?" Sokai asked.

"I have no idea," Indy said.

"No, I mean the entries," Sokai said impatiently. "They tell the past, present, and future? Find my entry and read it to me. If I know what lies ahead, then I can bend things to my will."

"All right," Indy said, stepping up to the book.

He slowly turned the pages.

"Hurry," Sokai said.

"This isn't easy to read," Indy said.

Musashi grabbed Mystery by the hair, close to the skull, and twisted. Mystery choked down the pain.

"I'm going as fast as I can," Indy said, his eyes smoldering. "Sokai, born in Hawaii. Schooled at—"

"I know all that," Sokai said. "Go on to the future."

"Nineteen thirty-four," Indy said. "Blinded in Manchuria by an American he was torturing. Followed the same American, Indiana Jones, from Manchuria to India and eventually to Egypt."

Indy paused.

"Go on!"

"If you insist," he said. *"Burned to death beneath the Great Pyramid in the Hall of Records at the Giza necropolis."*

"No!"

"That's what it says."

Sokai backhanded Indy with his fist.

"You are lying," Sokai said.

Indy wiped the blood from his split lower lip with the sleeve of his jacket and gave Sokai a hard look that convinced the spymaster that he wasn't.

"Change it," Sokai said.

"I can't," Indy protested. "I don't even know how it was written in the first place."

"Use a pencil," Sokai screamed. "You have a pencil, don't you?"

Indy took the pencil from his shirt pocket and tried to write on the page.

"It won't make a mark," Indy said.

"Try harder this time," Sokai said, "or Musashi will kill the girl."

Musashi switched the sword to her left hand, drew her pistol, cocked it, and held it to Mystery's head. Indy leaned so hard on the pencil trying to make a mark that it snapped.

Sokai grasped the page and tried to tear it from the book, but it wouldn't come loose. He succeeded only in slicing his hand on the edge of the page.

"Look," Musashi said.

Sokai's trouser leg, above the heel that had stamped out the torch, was beginning to smoke.

"My God, it's true," Indy said.

"No," Sokai said as the cuff burst into flames. He frantically tried to put the fire out, and when that didn't work he unbuckled his belt and tried to wriggle out of his pants. By this time, however, the flames had spread to his shirt and trench coat.

Sokai screamed. The room was filled with the stench of burning flesh and hair. Sokai dropped to the floor and began to roll.

"Cut them off me," he begged Musashi.

She dropped the pistol and attempted to slice the clothes away from his body, but succeeded only in stabbing him in a half dozen places. His very body seemed to be combusting, and the flames grew no matter how many articles of clothing were removed.

"My sword," Sokai croaked and grasped the handle with a burning hand. "I will at least take Jones with me."

Sokai struggled to his knees and made a lunge for Indy, but it was far too short. Pieces of burning flesh sloughed from his face and hands. Sokai fell upon his back, but held the blade aloft until the fire burned through his wrist and the samurai sword clattered onto the granite floor.

"Oh, God," Mystery said and went to Indy, where she buried her face against his leather jacket.

Sokai was nothing but a smoking pile of ashes.

"Want me to read your name?" he threatened Musashi.

She hesitated, then knelt beside the ashes. She removed her scarf and used it to pick up the samurai sword.

"Aren't you going to take his ashes?" Indy asked. "Or don't you care if he joins his ancestors?"

"To hell with Sokai," Musashi said and shook the sword at them. "This is the power!"

Then she ran from the room, and as she left the wavering music came again—except now it was an ominous, diminished chord. The lighting changed from white to red.

"I don't like the sound of that," Indy said.

"My mother," Mystery said, alarmed.

"Let's get out of here," Indy said.

"But my father—"

"Come on," he said as he pulled Mystery out of the Hall of Truth.

11

MIRACLES AND MAYHEM

Storm clouds hugged the eastern sky as Indy and Mystery emerged from the shaft between the Sphinx's paws. Faye and Sallah were kneeling on the ground, a pair of soldiers behind them with their guns pointing between their shoulder blades. Jadoo was standing in front of Faye, shaking his fist at her.

"This is not the Staff of Aaron," the magician said. "It does not work."

"It works," Faye said calmly.

"I'm sorry, Indy," Sallah said. "I tried to warn you—"

"It's all right," Indy said as a Japanese soldier took his whip and revolver from his belt.

"Shoot them!" Musashi said.

"No," Jadoo said. "We may need them."

"Who are you to give orders?" Musashi challenged.

"Sokai's dead," Jadoo said. "That puts me in command."

"Sokai Sensei is dead?" Miyamoto asked.

"Yes," Indy said. "He burned to death. The lieutenant has his sword."

Miyamoto turned to Musashi. She showed him the sword, and he clasped his hands together and gave a curt bow.

"*Hai*," he said. "Musashi Sensei is in charge."

"It was the American's fault," Musashi said quickly.

"That's not true," Mystery pleaded.

"It is true! He tricked him by twisting the words in the book!" Musashi said.

"You found the Omega Book?" Faye asked.

"Yes, they found it," Musashi said. "But they used it to kill Sokai Sensei. They must die."

The soldiers aimed their weapons at Indy.

"No," Miyamoto said as he unbuttoned his tunic. "Do not shoot him. I want the satisfaction of killing him with my bare hands."

"Don't kill the girl until her mother has shown me how to use the Staff," Jadoo said.

"If you're going to kill her anyway," Faye asked, "why should I show you at all?"

"To buy her a few more minutes of life," Jadoo

said. "And the chance that the bloodthirsty little lieutenant may change her mind. You help me, and I'll try to persuade her to let both of you go."

"I don't care about the women," Miyamoto said as he threw his shirt down. Even in the moonlight, Indy could see the muscles in his arms and chest bulging. "But the man, he is mine."

Faye nodded.

Jadoo handed her the Staff, and she struggled to her feet.

"Faye, don't believe him," Indy said.

Miyamoto threw a left jab, which Indy blocked, but he wasn't quick enough to deflect the pistonlike right that drove into his stomach, knocking the air out of him and sending him to his knees.

"Get up and fight, you cowardly American."

Indy held a finger up.

Miyamoto kicked him in the chest.

Indy flew backward and landed against the stelae.

Miyamoto advanced. Indy scrambled to his feet and punched him as hard as he could in the solar plexus, but Miyamoto just smiled and drove the knuckles of his right hand into Indy's jaw.

Indy went down again, and this time his mouth was filled with blood and the sickening feeling of a broken tooth loose in his mouth. He got back to his feet while spitting part of a bloody molar into the sand.

As he looked at the tooth, his mind spontaneously thought of the Old Testament admonition about "an eye for an eye, a tooth for a tooth," and that led his mind to the story of Exodus and the battles the Israelites fought. . . .

"Faye," Indy mumbled. "The Staff—"

Miyamoto hit him again in the stomach, and as Indy was doubled over, the Japanese sergeant drove a hammerlike fist into the back of his head. Indy jerked and went down to one knee. He punched Miyamoto in the thigh, and the sergeant groaned in pain and stumbled away.

Indy tried to capitalize on the opening, but by the time he had closed the distance Miyamoto was ready again and pummeled his face with a series of jabs.

"Indy!" Faye shouted. "What can I do?"

It suddenly came to him.

"Hold it up," Indy mumbled.

"What?"

Indy took two more punches to the body.

"Hold the Staff up," Indy pleaded. "As long as Moses held the Staff up, the Israelites could not lose in battle."

Faye tentatively raised the Staff.

Indy caught Miyamoto's next punch in his right hand, then drove Miyamoto's wrist backward until he fell to his knees and cried in pain. Miyamoto wrenched his injured hand away and threw two more punches with his other hand, which Indy blocked.

"Give it to him," Mystery shouted.

Indy stepped forward and shot two jabs to Miyamoto's jaw, then sent a right crashing into the space between his nose and upper lip. Miyamoto fell to the sand and spat out his front teeth.

"Take that!" Sallah said.

"Have you had enough?" Indy asked.

Miyamoto held up an open hand.

Musashi stepped forward.

"You idiot," she told Jadoo. "Take the Staff away from the woman." Jadoo grabbed the Staff, and he and Faye fought for control of it.

"Get in there and finish him," Musashi shouted at Miyamoto.

The Warrant Officer shook his head.

"You're pathetic," she said and, in one motion, drew Sokai's sword and lopped off Miyamoto's head.

Mystery screamed.

Then Musashi turned, her face flecked with her comrade's blood, and came at Indy.

She was so fast that Indy hardly had time to react as he saw the point of the razor-sharp blade coming toward his solar plexus. He managed to deflect most of the thrust by bringing the leather sleeve of his jacket against the flat of the blade, but he watched as the blade pierced the right side of his jacket.

Indy was stunned.

"I don't feel anything," he said.

"You will," Musashi said, twisting the blade.

Pain shot through Indy's side as blood stained his jacket.

Faye hit Jadoo in the mouth with the end of the Staff as he stared at the sword piercing Indy's side. Then she held the Rod aloft once more. When Jadoo made a grab for it again, she kicked him in the groin.

Indy backed away from the now-bloody blade, and it fell into the sand as if it were too heavy for Musashi to hold. Indy stepped forward with his right foot and brought it down on the sword.

It snapped in two.

Musashi threw the hilt away and drew her pistol. Indy flinched, expecting a slug between the eyes. But when the pistol fired, Indy heard the bullet ricochet off the stone tablet behind him.

"How could I miss?" Musashi asked.

A drop of blood ran down the side of her nose.

The bullet had ricocheted off the stelae and struck her between the eyes. She touched the fingers of her left hand to the blood and examined them, then her eyes rolled back in her head as she fell at Indy's feet.

"No," Indy said.

Mystery knelt down and felt for a pulse.

"Is she—"

"As a doornail," Mystery said as she turned to Indy. "She got what she deserved. Do you know how many times she nearly killed *us*?"

"Still," Indy said.

She unzipped his jacket and looked carefully inside.

"I'm stabbed," Indy said incredulously.

"You're bleeding pretty badly," she said.

"I hate swords," Indy complained.

"But it went through the fleshy part of your side," Mystery said as she tore material from the sleeve of her blouse and stuffed it inside his jacket. "Good thing you have a lot of fat there, because I don't think it pierced anything vital."

"Thanks a lot," he said.

"You idiots," Jadoo told the soldiers. "Get the stick!"

The soldiers gave him a dubious look that asked, "And end up like Miyamoto?"

"Faye," Jadoo pleaded. "Let me have the Staff of Aaron and show me how to use it. I'll let all of you go."

"Don't trust him," Indy said.

"Why not?" Faye asked. "We still have soldiers with guns pointed at us."

"He killed Kaspar," Indy blurted.

"What?" Mystery asked.

Storm clouds passed in front of the moon.

"I'm sorry," Indy said. "I didn't want to tell you, but that's what the book said. Jadoo poisoned him when he came to see him in 1930, decapitated the body, and used the skull for a drinking glass. I'm sorry, Faye, but that was Kaspar's skull we saw on his shelf in Calcutta."

"I suspected as much," Faye said sadly.

The wind whipped her hair in front of her face. As a single tear rolled down her cheek, it began to sprinkle.

A frog plopped down at Jadoo's feet and hopped away.

"Did you see that?" Mystery asked.

Then it began to rain in earnest. Another frog fell on the brim of Indy's hat, and then came a barrage of the amphibians, thudding into the sand and scampering away.

"What is this?" Jadoo asked.

"Don't you know?" Indy asked with delight. "It's a plague."

The soldiers lowered their rifles.

Jadoo screamed at them, and they came back to attention.

"This is not unknown," Jadoo stammered. "It's rained frogs before, as anybody who's read Charles

Fort's *Book of the Damned* knows. This is no plague, just a freak of nature."

"Oh, no?" Faye asked.

She spread her arms, the Staff held in her right hand, and turned her face to the sky.

"*Hail*," she commanded.

A bolt of lightning struck the head of the Sphinx, showering them all with sparks and leaving their ears ringing. The lightning was followed by chunks of flaming, baseball-sized hail that covered the sand.

The soldiers dropped their guns and put their hands over their heads for protection. Jadoo shouted at them, but they refused to pick up their weapons.

Indy pulled Mystery close to him, while Jadoo cowered and Sallah looked around in amazement.

"Faye," Indy shouted as a flaming hailstone thumped him on the back. "This is bad."

Faye nodded. She turned her face skyward and announced, "*Blood!*"

The rain turned dark.

"Oh, my God," Mystery said as she touched her fingers to her mouth. "It's real."

The soldiers abandoned their weapons and ran, leaving Jadoo behind.

"Faye, end this," Indy pleaded.

Faye glared at Jadoo.

"A curse," she said.

"No," he pleaded and fell to his knees, his hands together. "I beg you for mercy."

"Did you show mercy to my husband?"

"I didn't kill him," Jadoo lied. "You don't understand the circumstances. It wasn't my fault."

"Death," Faye pronounced, "to the seventh born, of the seventh born—"

"No!" Indy shouted. "That includes Sallah!"

"—of the seventh born."

"Okay," Indy said and shrugged.

Jadoo's eyes became wild. He got to his feet and backed away from Faye, then began to run. Then he fell gasping to the ground, holding his chest. He died of a massive coronary, with his eyes open and his heels digging into the sand.

Faye looked at the carnage around her.

She hoisted the Staff like a javelin and threw it. It sailed in a great arc for two hundred yards and buried itself in the sand, not far from the Nile.

"It is finished," Sallah said.

"Almost," Indy said.

"The scavengers will finish what is left of these villians before the day becomes hot," Sallah said. "They deserve nothing better."

"No," Indy said, holding his side. "We must bury them. But there is one other thing we must do—we've got to seal this entrance. Come help me push the stone into place. Then we will fill the hole with sand, and it will be safe for many more years."

"But the book," Sallah said. "You found it, no?"

"We found it, yes," Indy said.

"The world isn't ready for it," Mystery added.

"She's right," Indy said. "She's always been right. And the prophecies about the Hall of Records are true as well: that the world will not learn of their discovery until years after they have been located."

"But Indy," Sallah said. "If not now, when?"

"When it's time, my friend," Indy said. "When it's time."

12

THE CRYSTAL SKULL

The taxi pulled to a stop in front of the apartment building and honked. Indy emerged, wearing a new suit, but with his favorite fedora on his head. He was followed by Sallah and his pack of children. Indy and Sallah shook hands, and then Sallah pulled him to his chest and engulfed him in a bear hug.

"I need to ask a favor," Indy said when he could breathe again.

"Anything."

"The next time we meet," Indy said, "let's not speak of what occurred here beneath the Giza plateau, or mention this to Marcus Brody. Let's not tempt ourselves to reveal this before the world is ready, or time will be out of joint. I can't explain it, just trust me."

"As you wish, my friend," Sallah said.

"Where are Faye and Mystery?" Indy asked. "I thought they would be here."

"They left early this morning," Sallah said. "They are on their way back to the United States. But they left this for you."

Sallah handed Indy a letter.

"Thanks," Indy said.

"Farewell, my friend," Sallah said. "It was a grand adventure. But the next time, let's choose something a little less dangerous."

Indy grinned, but said nothing.

He got in the taxi, then touched his finger to the brim of his hat as it pulled away.

"Where to?"

"The airport," Indy said.

As the taxi bounced along, he opened the letter and read it.

Dear Indy,
Sorry Mother and I aren't there to see you off,
but we are superstitious about good-byes.
Thanks for all of your help in finding out
what happened to Father. I was devastated to
learn he was dead, but glad to know the truth.

Mother says that even though magic works,
it operates by its own quirky set of rules, and
is no substitute for reality; it cannot, for

example, bring back the ones we love. I think, however, that all real magic comes from God, whose rules make us work for the things we want so we don't get spoiled.

We're going home to Oklahoma, where mother expects me to finish up high school. Ugh! How can I go back to school when I've stood on the Sphinx, survived two shipwrecks, nearly been turned into a mummy, and witnessed real miracles? The worst part is that nobody will ever believe me about the Omega Book and the frogs and the blood and stuff. Oh, well. At least we know it's true, right?

Take care of yourself. I don't know what our address will be, but if I send it to you in care of Princeton University, will you please write?

Your friend,
Mysti

P.S. I had a crush on you, but I got over it.

Indy arrived at Princeton a week later.

It was a drowsy Saturday afternoon, and the university seemed deserted. On the fourth floor of McCormick Hall, in the Department of Art and Archaeology, he stood for a moment in front of the door to his office, startled for a moment by his reflection in the windowpane. He had been without the company of his reflection for most of the spontaneous Omega Book expedition, because few of the places he had been in the last few weeks were stocked with mirrors. Now that he had a chance to get a good look at himself again, it seemed as if a stranger stared back: thinner than he remembered, badly in need of a shave and a haircut, and with lines in his face that were more than just products of wind and sun.

Indy shook his head and tried the doorknob. It was, of course, locked. He absently patted his suit pockets while trying to remember where he had left his keys for safekeeping. At home? Or with Marcus Brody? He was about to smash the windowpane with his elbow—partly out of frustration, and partly out of discomfort with the image of himself he'd just seen—when he noticed a janitor at the end of the hall.

"Pardon me," Indy said, "but I'm a pro—"

"Dr. Jones," the man said. "I know who you are."

"Your name is—"

"Arthur."

"Right," Indy said with a smile. "The trouble is, I've locked myself out of my office. I wonder if you would mind opening the door for me?"

"Dr. Jones," Arthur said. "You never leave your keys at home. I'm surprised."

"Yeah," Indy said and smiled. "I'm just not myself today."

"You look a little tired," Arthur agreed.

The janitor opened the door with a key from the ring at his belt, and Indy stepped inside. "Thanks," he said as he closed the door.

There was the usual pile of mail on his desk—alongside a stack of papers to be graded—and on the top of the pile was a first-class letter postmarked from Claremore, Oklahoma. He slipped the letter into his jacket pocket.

Beneath the letter from Mystery was an official-looking one from Barnett College, which he knew had to be a job offer. He considered opening it, but returned it to the stack. Then he turned to the shelves and found, behind some books, a three-gallon glass specimen jar filled with denatured alcohol.

He took the jar down, placed it on the desk, and removed the lid. Then he took off his jacket and rolled up a shirtsleeve. The jar appeared to be empty except for the alcohol.

He reached inside the jar, felt around, hooked two fingers in the eye sockets of the Crystal Skull, and drew it out. The jaw hung open, giving the impression that the skull was screaming, and rainbows of light danced in the orbital sockets. It was still as frightening as the day years ago that he'd found it in the Temple of the Serpent, beneath the lost city of Cozan, in British Honduras.

The skull had been the occult prize in a deadly game of cat-and-mouse over the years, and Indy had alternately won and lost it several times. The skull had traveled across Europe, sunk to the bottom of the sea, and been recovered in the Arctic. And, as with most great treasures, it came with a curse: that whoever removed it from the altar in the Temple of the Serpent would kill what he loved best. And although Indy did not believe in curses, he had watched Alecia Dunstin die, under circumstances for which he felt responsible. Their relationship had been fated since the day they'd met in the library of the British Museum. If they hadn't met, Indy believed, the beautiful and clairvoyant Englishwoman would still be alive. Sometimes, when Indy closed his eyes for sleep, the image of her face would come to him.

Indy looked at a generic bank calendar that hung on the wall, its big red letters marking a row of Sundays. Every day should be marked in red, Indy thought, to remind us that each day is precious, and to warn against wasting a single one.

Indy held the skull in both hands, elevated it to eye level, and turned its vacant sockets toward him.

"I've lost enough because of you," Indy told the skull.

A bluish shimmer danced across its teeth, while a sudden chill shot through Indy's palms. He optimistically attributed both effects to the rapidly evaporating alcohol. Indy usually avoided touching the skull with his bare hands, but for some reason he had a need for direct contact with the cold quartz; perhaps, he told himself, he simply wanted to let it know that he was finally prepared to deal with it—come what might.

He would return the skull to the temple in the lost city where it had been discovered. And although that had been Indy's aim since recovering the skull in the Arctic, something had always seemed to intervene, and Indy had hidden the skull in the jar of alcohol on his office shelf. The specific gravity of the alcohol was nearly the same as quartz crystal, and rendered the skull invisible. Although his office had been rifled several times, the skull had not been found.

He placed the skull on his desk.

The phone rang.

Indy stared at it for a moment, debating whether to answer it. Finally, acting on a feeling he could not explain, he picked up the receiver.

"Hello, Indy?" a familiar voice asked. "Is that you?"

"Marcus?" Indy asked.

"Yes, of course. I'm glad I caught you. I tried earlier calling at your home."

"Haven't been back there yet," Indy said and sat down.

"Just got back and had to check into work, eh?" Brody asked.

"Just tying up some loose ends."

"Say, the strangest thing happened while you've been gone. Some chap claiming to be you wired the museum from India asking for a thousand U.S. dollars. I knew you were in China, but I wired the money anyway, on the remote chance it really was you and you were truly in need. Anyway, the bloke got away with the cash, it seems."

"That bloke was me," Indy asked.

"Really?" Brody asked. "What were you up to in Calcutta?"

"The usual," Indy replied. "On my way to someplace else. Wound up at Giza digging—"

"No, don't tell me," Brody interrupted. "I'm sure your actions were strictly professional and in accordance with international law and the guidelines of the Service des Antiquités."

"You might say my authorization came from the highest authority."

"Splendid. By the way, a package came to the

museum today from Cairo. It's addressed to you, and the return address—if I can decipher the scrawl—seems to be from your friend Sallah. Could this be spoils of your adventure? May I open it?"

Before Indy could reply, he could hear the sound of tearing paper on the other end.

"It's a box of almonds," Brody said with more than a little disappointment. "There's a note attached. It says: *Not breaking any promises, but thought you would like to know that where the stick landed, an almond tree now blooms. Until we meet again, my friend.*"

Indy laughed.

"There must be a story behind that," Brody said.

"There is," Indy said.

"And I'm sure someday you'll tell me," Brody said. "Oh, one last thing, and the real reason I called. Have you ever heard of something called the ashes of Nurhachi?"

"Yes," Indy said, "but I'd like to rest before I go to Shanghai chasing after them. Also, I've got a job offer that I need to consider. I may be changing colleges soon."

"Excellent," Brody said. "Oh, to be a young man again. You rest up, and give me a ring when you've decided."

"I will," Indy said. "Marcus?"

"What is it?"

For a moment Indy's throat was so dry he could not speak. Finally, he said:

"It's good to hear your voice again, Marcus."

"Are you all right?" Brody asked. "Nothing is wrong, is it?"

"No," Indy said. "I'm fine. Or, at least I will be."

13

TIME OUT OF JOINT

Indy planted the torch in the mud in front of the empty altar and took a pair of leather gloves from his pocket. His face was covered in mud and sweat, and his bruised hands ached as he snugged the gloves over them. The descent into the cavern beneath the Temple of the Serpent had been as difficult and as dangerous as he remembered it, but with an important exception: There was no giant snake this time. Shattered bones from the thirty-foot anaconda Indy had killed years earlier littered the banks of the subterranean pool.

Indy retrieved the bulky velvet bag from the satchel slung over his shoulder, and from the bag he removed the Crystal Skull. The light of the torch was refracted and magnified in the depths of the skull, and danced across the floor and walls of the cavern. For a moment Indy was mesmerized by the display, and he considered keeping the skull.

"No," he said aloud. "I don't know who you were—or are—but this is where you belong."

The altar was cut into an alcove in the wall of the cavern. Indy planted his feet firmly on the ground, made sure he had his balance, and carefully placed the skull atop the altar. Then he stepped back, half expecting some trap to spring out of the base of the altar or to fall from above.

"Good," Indy said.

He smiled, took off his gloves, and touched the brim of his hat in farewell. Then, when he picked up his torch and turned to leave, he heard it: a swirl of water, a slithering noise from the mud bank, and the awful hissing sound of a very large snake breathing. At the far end of the torch's circle of light he saw an amber, slitted eye the size of a cantaloupe moving toward him.

The snake he had killed in this cavern before had been the largest one he had ever seen, and when he'd returned to Princeton he had asked a herpetologist if anacondas of thirty feet in length were unheard of. No, the expert had said, there were tales of them growing even bigger in the depths of the rain forest.

This snake made the other one seem small.

"Not again," Indy moaned.

The snake slithered toward him.

Indy drew the revolver.

There was no place to run; the snake was so long that it completely cut off the route back to the entrance to the subterranean pool, and to try to swim would be surrendering an even greater advantage to the snake.

Indy stumbled backward and fired three rounds at the snake's eye. If it had any effect, the snake did not show it. The snake opened its hinged jaw—showing fangs that were as big as sabers—and flicked its spongy pink tongue toward Indy. Like all snakes, its eyesight was bad, but its senses of smell and taste were keen.

Indy squeezed into the alcove beside the altar and fired twice more. The snake struck, but its open mouth was larger than the alcove, and the fangs grated against rock.

Flinching from the strike, Indy threw himself backward and hit his head on the lintel of a stone portal in the back of the alcove. Because the portal was small—less than five feet high—and in the shadows behind the altar, he had not noticed it before. More important, the portal was too small for the snake to come through.

It was a moment, however, before Indy realized this. The blow to the back of the head had nearly rendered him unconscious, and for a few minutes he sat on the floor of this new passage while his stomach churned and pinwheels of light danced in front of his eyes. When he felt the back of his head, there was blood on his hand.

Still, Indy smiled at his good fortune.

He picked up the torch and struggled to his feet to explore this new passage and get away from the angry hissing on the other side of the portal. The ceiling was low, and he had to stoop as he inched along.

Then the passage ended.

It ended not in a doorway, or a wall, or even the rubble of a collapse. It ended in a kind of cloud filled with darkness that was beyond darkness, a malevolent void that refused to be dispelled by torchlight. Instead, it seemed to soak up the light and yield nothing in return. And, it was growing—or simply coming toward him.

Indy searched the corridor for a recognizable doorway, or a crawl space, or some exit that was an alternative to *whatever* was in front of him and the angry and very large snake behind.

There was none.

Indy switched the torch to his left hand, then extended the fingers of his right. Carefully, he touched the cloud. His hand disappeared in the void, but there was no sensation of feeling—not even the feel of his fingers tucking into his palm as he made a fist.

He quickly drew back his arm, and was relieved to find that his hand was still attached.

Indy glanced behind him, then looked around at the barren corridor again. Of the three choices open to him, two offered certain death: starving to death in the bowels of the temple, or being crushed in the coils of a giant anaconda. Although the third choice seemed only to suggest disaster instead of promising it, he was hesitant to take it. But as the cloud began to envelop him in wispy hollow tendrils, his torch began to dim and then sputter. Afraid that he would be suffocated like the flame if he did not push on through the cloud to the other side, he held his breath and plunged into it.

He found himself in sunshine.

I must have hit my head harder than I realized, Indy said to himself, rubbing his neck and blinking against the brilliance of daylight. Then he closed his eyes and opened them again.

As his eyes slowly adjusted, the outlines of the city of Cozan rose around him. Indy was kneeling on the bottom step of the Temple of the Serpent. Birds and monkeys were thick in the nearby trees, and somewhere a jaguar growled.

Only, this was not the corpse of a city that Indy remembered finding—this was a living metropolis, and it was still in its youth. People filled the streets and moved in the shadows of buildings that Indy had seen only as heaping ruins amid the encroaching jungle. The structures were magnificent limestone monuments, trimmed in green and terracotta. The number of buildings, however, were fewer than the ruins of modern-day Cozan would indicate there to have been. Behind him was the Temple of the Serpent, but it was smaller—it was much lower and had fewer courses than he could recall.

Indy stepped down from the temple onto the broad flagstones of the busy main thoroughfare. Although he gaped at the people he passed—robust, brown-skinned people dressed mostly in tunics made from fibers of the maguey plant—none of them so much as returned Indy's stare.

Many of them hastily bartered corn, fruit, and spitted meat at the thatch-covered stalls on either side of the street, while others seemed to be nervously awaiting some event. They glanced up at the sky from time to time, or noted the diminishing length of their shadows on the flagstones with the same expression as a businessman on Wall Street would glance at his wristwatch.

The sun was almost overhead.

Whatever event was being anticipated, it was obvious that it would take place at noon.

Although here in British Honduras one would expect to find Mayans, Indy mused, these people had the sharper features of the Aztecs of Central

Mexico. Yet, there were none of the easily recognizable trademarks of Aztec culture. Indy could not identify their speech, but he knew it was not Nahuatl, the language of the Aztecs. The predominant feature of the glyphs that decorated the Cozanian monuments was a stylized spiral that unwound to the right; it could be a representation of the conch shell, Indy thought, or perhaps a star or comet. Nothing was known of the history of Cozan, except that it had once been a great city but had been abandoned because of some evil, and even that came from folklore; before Indy had discovered the city for himself, he'd doubted its existence.

The city's name, Cozan, was borrowed from a sixteenth-century translation of a little-understood Mayan phrase in which the Spanish word for heart, *corazón*, figured prominently. Sometimes it was rendered as *del mal corazón*, or heartless; at other times the Mayan place name for the lost city defied translation, but the closest one would be the "heart of evil."

The warriors, who seemed to be everywhere, carried obsidian blades at their belts and, slung over their shoulders, wicked-looking throwing sticks made from oak branches. They strolled the avenue in pairs and occasionally stopped to warn a merchant or a citizen that they should be finishing their business, because the ceremony was about to start.

The class distinctions went far beyond warrior and citizen, Indy discovered. Another class made up at least a third of the population. Their faces were dusted with blue powder, making them appear like ghosts following behind their masters and mistresses. Their eyes were vacant, devoid of hope, and Indy guessed why: Blue is the color of sacrifice.

Indy had often dealt with the remains of sacrificial victims, and with few exceptions they had always seemed to submit themselves willingly for the good of the community, often after a period of a year or so in which they were treated like heroes and honored as royalty. Even when their hands were bound behind their backs, or when a ligature was found around the vertebrae of their necks, there were indications that they had submitted voluntarily, rather than having been murdered. These slaves, who were apparent war prizes, were not looking forward to their contribution to the great chain of being.

"Excuse me," Indy said, going from one citizen to another.

"Pardon me, may I have a moment?" Apparently, none of them could see or hear him.

Indy reached out to touch a passing warrior, and the man jumped back as if he had been stung where Indy's fingers had made contact with his arm.

Convinced he had been bitten by an insect, he waved a hand in front of his face and kept moving.

Then, at the sound of a conch shell trumpet, the throng fled the center of the street and took up positions along each side. The blue-faced slaves fell to their knees and lowered their foreheads to the ground. The warriors stood at attention, obsidian-tipped spears at the ready.

A shaman crab-walked toward the pyramid, dusting the street with a branch. In his other hand he held a mace made from a human thighbone with a smooth river rock lashed to the end. He was nude except for a breechcloth, and elaborately tattooed with the nationalistic right-facing spirals Indy had already seen on the glyphs. He wore a gruesome mask made from the front half of a human skull and decorated with jade and obsidian. Sticking like a rhino's horns from the forehead and nasal cavity were two wicked-looking flint points.

This monster with a human hidden beneath often rushed the crowd, shaking the mace at them and driving them back in terror. Whatever god of death or destruction this joker was supposed to represent, Indy decided, the citizens obviously believed he was the real deal.

Indy tapped him on the shoulder and was delighted to see the medicine man spring backward, alarmed at an apparent manifestation of *real* magic.

He savagely shook his mace in Indy's direction, but kept moving toward the temple.

Following the shaman was a phalanx of priests, dressed in cotton tunics dyed in terra-cotta and green and emblazoned with the Cozanian spirals. The center priest carried a hat-sized oak box in his hands.

Behind the priests, on a litter borne by slaves, came a strikingly beautiful woman. She wore a simple cotton gown, and was unadorned with jewelry or any other sign of class or authority. She was tall, perhaps six feet, and the muscles in her exposed arms and calves suggested that she was athletic. She reminded Indy of a jaguar because of her sleek black hair and broad face and her liquid green eyes.

Their eyes seemed to meet as the litter swayed past.

For a moment, Indy was sure that she had seen him. Her expression was one of puzzlement and alarm, and she sat up and looked over her shoulder at the spot where the stranger had stood. This time, however, her eyes searched the crowd without finding him.

Behind the litter limped a half dozen blue-faced slaves driven by a group of soldiers. The slaves were of both genders, young and old, and their feet were bound with a length of rope, which was just long enough to allow them to walk, but no more. As they shuffled past the crowd threw garbage at them and shouted insults. The children in attendance were encouraged to dash out and swat at the slaves with sticks. They did so with glee, then raced back to the protection of their mothers' legs.

When the procession reached the bottom step of the pyramid, the litter was gently placed on the ground. The Queen stepped from her throne with the grace and agility of a big cat, then proceeded to climb the steps. She was followed by the priests and the others, and finally the rest of the city surged onto the pyramid. Indy followed along with the flow of the crowd up the side of the pyramid, and when he reached the apex he was astonished to find not a temple but a concave area containing a sacred well. In twenty or thirty centuries, course after course would be added to the pyramid and this area would actually become the subterranean pool at the bottom of the Temple of the Serpent.

The high priest placed the wooden box he carried on a stone altar and lifted the Crystal Skull from it. It looked as finished as the day Indy had discovered it. The priest held the skull aloft, and the crowd averted their eyes as the sunlight gathered in the prisms behind the eye sockets and shot dancing rainbows of light over their heads. Only the Queen— and, of course, Indy—did not look away. Then the priest began speaking in a ritual monotone, and

Indy guessed that he was reciting a history of the skull. The skull-masked shaman went into a pantomime. Although Indy did not understand one word of the speech, from the playacting Indy guessed that *they* had found the skull in the jungle one day as well, perhaps at the bottom of a sacred well or a cave littered with the bones of unimaginably old human sacrifices. Since that time, the skull had apparently become the state religion, a religion based on war and conquest—and an unquenchable appetite for human sacrifice.

Fascists, Indy said to himself. I hate these guys.

As the priests concluded the recitation, another of the priests removed the wooden box and the Crystal Skull was placed on the stone altar, gazing out over the sacred pool. As the high priest began to chant a sacred song, the Queen waded into the pool, her arms outstretched. Her cotton gown swirled around her. Then, when she was chest-high in the water, she stopped and placed her hands atop her head.

Something moved in the water around her.

A pair of anacondas wrapped themselves around her torso and lifted their heads from the water. They were not big snakes as anacondas go—they were perhaps twelve or fifteen feet in length—but at any moment Indy expected to hear the cracking of her rib cage as the snakes squeezed the life out of her.

Instead, the snakes serpentined around the

Queen's torso like a pair of tame cats. The Queen's mouth went slack, and her eyelids fluttered in religious ecstasy.

Then the snakes left her and made instead for the bank of the pool, where the slave sacrifices knelt beneath the obsidian blades of the warriors.

"Hey!" Indy shouted, moving closer. "Get up! Get out of there! At least make a run for it."

Indy pulled out the Webley, drew a careful bead on the head of the larger of the snakes, and fired. The Webley barked, but the slug did no damage. He squeezed off the remaining rounds in the cylinder, but there was not so much as a splash of water behind the snake to indicate that a slug had even been fired.

The snakes took the closest victim first. They slithered up his legs, wrapped themselves around his abdomen, and began to squeeze the life out of him while he shook with fear. When they were finished with him, they rolled him into the cenote, the sacred pool. Then they went to the next in line and began to repeat the process.

"Fight!" Indy said. "Why don't you fight?"

One of the slaves in the middle of the sacrificial line, a powerfully built young woman whose mouth was still swollen from a recent beating, kept her head down but watched the approach of the snakes from beneath half-closed lids. Indy saw her take a deep breath, watched the muscles in her arms and legs tense, and helplessly shouted encouragement when she turned and sent a knee into the groin of the warrior who guarded her.

The soldier gasped and the slave girl snatched the obsidian sword from his grasp. In one two-handed movement she brought the blade slashing up against his throat, nearly decapitating him. As the guard's body fell to the ground she released a war cry that was so alarming the birds fled the surrounding trees.

She slashed the ropes that bound her ankles. But instead of racing down the steps of the pyramid toward freedom, she turned instead in the direction of the high priest. She plunged the blade into his stomach, then leaped into the cenote and splashed frantically toward the Queen. Although the sun was now hidden by a cloud, the Crystal Skull blazed even more fiercely than before.

The Queen smiled and opened her arms as if to embrace her.

Then a half dozen baseball-sized stones struck the slave girl's body, propelled with mechanical force by the warriors with the heavy sticks. The stones broke bones wherever they struck her body: her back, her ribs, her left arm. But despite these injuries, she maintained her forward motion and managed to draw the sword with her unbroken right arm.

The slave girl was about to bring it down upon

the smiling Queen's head when a last stone struck the base of her skull, and all life went out of her body. The sword fell impotently into the water. She fell facedown in the water, with a growing rose-colored bloom around her head.

Indy turned away.

The Crystal Skull glowed so brightly on the stone altar that it seemed on fire. Then, the jaw dropped and a black cloud began issuing from its mouth.

Indy's vision blurred as the cloud engulfed him.

When he could see again, he was standing in front of the heaping ruins of the Temple of Serpent. The jungle was once more in command. But on the ground at his feet was a granite rock the size of a baseball, covered with hair and fresh blood.

Epilogue

He found the professor on the Quadrangle, sitting on a bench in the sunshine, eating a sandwich from a sack lunch beside him. The man was just past fifty, but already he had the distracted mannerisms of age. Or, perhaps he had always had. His graying hair was a bird's nest of tangles. His clothes were rumpled and somewhat mismatched, and when he crossed his legs Indy noticed he wasn't wearing socks. As the professor slowly ate his sandwich, his unfocused eyes were fixed above the spires and rooftops of Princeton University.

Indy stood uncomfortably some yards from the bench, his fedora in his hands, unwilling to disturb the professor's apparent reverie. But the expectant, worried look on Indy's face was enough to warrant the older man's attention.

"Come," the professor finally said with a wave of his hand and a glance toward Indy. "Are you going to stand there all day or are you going to speak?"

"I didn't want to disturb you," Indy said sheepishly.

"And you think your staring is not disturbing?"

"Pardon me," Indy said. "It was rude."

Indy turned to go.

"Wait, wait," the older man said. "Come and sit beside me. I'm the one who is being rude now, I'm afraid. What is on your mind? Something interesting, I hope. Perhaps you are merely an autograph seeker? I do not understand this American obsession with fame."

"No, professor," Indy said as he sat down on the bench, his hat still in his hands. "I haven't come for your autograph, or for your picture. I've come for your advice."

"Advice," the man said and chuckled. "Everybody wants my advice these days. I'm afraid you have come to a very poor source for that. I have been accused of being a not very practical person, of spending too much time in my head and not enough time in the world. Do you know what I was thinking just now? I was thinking of how beautiful the clouds are, and how I would stare at them through the classroom window when I was a child."

"Did you like school?"

"I hated it," the professor said with a dismissive wave of his hand. "I wanted to be in the clouds. School was dull, regimented, and sucked the very life out of young minds. I was a very unhappy little boy. What a shame we do this to our young."

Indy smiled.

"The advice I seek," he said, "is of a very impractical nature."

"Have I seen you before?"

"Yes, sir. I teach archaeology here. My name is Jones, and we have met once or twice. My friend Marcus Brody introduced us."

"I'm sorry, but I don't remember," the professor said.

"I'm sure you had more important things on your mind."

"Like clouds," the professor said and smiled mischievously. Then he finished his sandwich, dusted the crumbs from his hands, and rummaged in his lunch sack. He extracted a bright red apple, which he offered to Indy.

Indy was hungry. He placed the fedora on the ground between his feet. Then he polished the apple on his pant leg, regarded the shine of the bright red skin for a moment, and sank his teeth into it.

"What is this very impractical advice you seek?"

"Time," Indy mumbled as he wiped apple juice from the corner of his mouth with the back of his hand. "Why is it always *now*? Is it possible to return to the past, or to move ahead to the future? What exactly is time, anyway?"

The professor smiled.

"Time," he said, "is what you measure with a clock."

Indy waited patiently.

"That's it?" he asked when he realized nothing more was forthcoming.

"What more do you want?" the professor asked.

"I don't know," Indy said. "Answers, I suppose. After all, you are the world's greatest authority."

The older man scowled.

"That is fate playing a trick on me," he said. "I have questioned authority all of my life, and now I find *myself* an authority."

Indy was disappointed.

"I was hoping you could give me some . . . validation," Indy said. "I have had some unusual experiences, in which miracles seemed possible. Time travel, even."

"You're asking me to tell you that you're not crazy," the professor said. "But I can't help you. I am merely a scientist, just another human being like yourself. The answers you seek, my son, are inside of you."

Indy nodded.

The professor smiled.

"One of the most incomprehensible things about the universe," the older man said, "is that we can comprehend it at all. But we are still in childhood, and as our understanding grows, so does our responsibility. We are all travelers in time, Dr. Jones. Live in the present, keep looking to the future, but always remember the past. And never forget to listen to your heart."

Afterword

Does magic work?

That question continues to nag, despite advances by science during the last three hundred years that would otherwise seem to lay the question to rest— with a resounding "No!"—once and for all. But the question is more than academic; it gets into the thorny area of belief, straddling the dark middle ground between superstition and religion.

There is a distinction between stage magic, which is used to entertain, and that which is done in an earnest attempt to influence natural or human events. Nobody makes that distinction clearer, or is more cynical of attempts at real magic, than professional magicians such as James Randi. Randi, through a foundation bearing his name, has a standing offer of more than a million dollars to anyone who can, on demand, demonstrate "any psychic, supernatural, or paranormal ability of any kind under satisfactory observing conditions." Although some have attempted, none have succeeded in winning the reward.

Randi's attitude, and that of the late Carl Sagan, author of *The Demon-Haunted World,* exemplifies the paradigm embraced by most scientists. If something cannot be verified by the experimental method, the hard line goes, then it does not exist. Anecdotal evidence that suggests the existence of ESP and other fringe beliefs is merely a manifestation of the human need to tell stories and sustain the understandable but childish habit of magical thinking. Indeed, there does appear to be a deep-rooted need for stories that perpetuate the belief in magic or otherworldly doings, as any researcher in "urban folklore" can tell you: Statues that weep blood, ghostly hitchhikers that disappear upon arrival at their destination, and alien beings that commit abductions with sexual overtones hark back to tales told in earlier centuries.

A somewhat softer attitude has been taken by researchers such as Rupert Sheldrake, author of *Seven Experiments That Could Change the World.* Sheldrake argues that ESP and other traditionally taboo topics have been neglected for too long by mainstream science. It is time, Sheldrake says, to test these phenomena on a wide scale, and it doesn't take big money in the form of endowments or research grants to do it.

"This book is not only about a more open kind of science," Sheldrake writes, "but about a more open way of *doing* science: more public, more participatory, less the monopoly of a scientific priesthood." He suggests seven shoestring experiments for the layperson to test—for example, the seemingly psychic ability of pigeons to home and the common human sensation of being stared at. About 80 percent of people have experienced the latter, Sheldrake says, and the phenomenon is closely related to the ancient "Evil Eye"—a belief in negative influence that can be transmitted to another by the act of staring.

Magic is a part of all religious systems, or appears to be at least a part of the *origins* of all religions, although its importance to each system varies. In the nineteenth century, however, there was a trend in Judeo-Christian civilization to set magic apart from other religious phenomena and to describe cultures that practiced it as "primitive." Today, the distinction between magic and religion is less clear, although magic tends to be technical and impersonal—a means to an end, in other words— while religion has personal and spiritual overtones.

Egypt was called the "cradle of magic" by Albert A. Hopkins in his 1897 book documenting the world's most famous magic tricks, and for good reason. In addition to Pharaoh's magicians mentioned in Exodus, ancient papyri are rife with spells and incantations, and there survive plenty of magical documents from the apex of Eygptian magic, which occurred around the second century in Alexandria. Indeed, magic—at least professional magic, the conjurer's art—seems to have survived well in the twentieth century. Snake charming is still a widespread family business from Egypt to India.

John A. Keel's *Jadoo,* first published in 1957, is an absorbing investigation into the "black magic of the Orient," and those interested in snake charmers, rope tricks, and abominable snowmen will find it delightful. Black magic, by the way, is that which is intended to harm another, and is also known as sorcery; white magic is said to be beneficial; and divination is an attempt to understand or foretell events rather than influence them. Stage magic, however, can be more clearly defined.

Jean Eugene Robert Houdin, the nineteenth-century French magician who is regarded as the father of modern stage magic, named five classes of performance magic, all of which are still with us in one form or another: Feats of Dexterity, such as card tricks and other legerdemains; Experiments in Natural Magic, which employ established scientific processes for entertainment; Mental Conjuring; Pretended

Mesmerism, such as "mind reading" acts and displays of extrasensory perception; and Pretended Mediumship, such as the classic nineteenth-century séance and its New Age counterpart, channeling.

Closely related to stage magic is the performance of the escape artist, which came into its own early in this century. The most famous of all escape artists was Harry Houdini, who was born Erik Weisz and adopted a stage name in honor of Robert Houdin. Like Randi, Houdini vigorously crusaded against mediums and others he considered frauds. Yet, the question lingered in the back of Houdini's mind, too: Was communication beyond the grave possible? Long before he died on Halloween, 1926, of a ruptured appendix, he had established a code to be delivered to his wife so that she would know if his spirit existed on the other side. The code was delivered to his wife during a séance, but there was later a suggestion that the medium may have learned of the code through a third party.

The nexus where magic and science meet is in the mind of the beholder. Ask any nontechnical person how a television set, or a computer, or a microwave works, and you are likely to get a blank stare and the rather pragmatic defense that the important thing is knowing how to use the devices, not understanding how they work. I am reminded of the maxim by scientist and science fiction writer Arthur C. Clarke:

"Any sufficiently advanced technology is indistinguishable from magic."

The Staff of Aaron

Like the Ark of the Covenant, the Staff is a biblical artifact that continues to resonate with the power, mystery, and sometimes vengeful and warlike spirit of the God of the Old Testament. It is also called the Staff of God in scripture, and is sometimes incorrectly identified in popular culture as belonging to Moses; although the Staff was the instrument that helped summon the plagues upon Egypt, and that mysteriously enabled the Hebrews to win in battle (as long as Moses held it up), this miraculous device actually belonged to Aaron. The story of Moses—who delivered his people from Egyptian slavery and established the independence of Israel as a nation in about 1440 B.C.—is incomplete without mention of Aaron, Moses' older brother, and their sister, Miriam.

Born three years before Pharaoh's edict to kill all male children, Aaron was the elder brother of Moses. His name means "uncertain" in Hebrew, and this seems to describe Aaron best; he was sometimes weak in character, and jealous. When Moses ascended Mount Sinai to receive the Ten Commandments directly from God, Aaron helped the backsliding Israelites return to idolatry by fashioning the golden calf. Aaron, along with his sister, who was a prophetess, was also harshly critical of Moses' marriage to a Cushitic woman. Yet, Aaron consistently found favor from the Lord. He, not Moses, was the supreme religious leader of the Israelites. When his authority as high priest was challenged, Aaron's staff miraculously bloomed and bore fruit, signifying his divine authority; his position was then made perpetual by the inclusion of the Staff in the Ark of the Covenant, along with the second pair of stone tablets (Moses had smashed the first in anger) containing the Ten Commandments. The Ark was the focus of the Israelites' traveling sanctuary, which, according to scripture, had the nasty habit of striking those dead who dared come near it.

When Moses first received his commission as a deliverer of his people, and doubted his ability to lead—perhaps because of a stutter or speech impediment, some say—Aaron was chosen by God to be his spokesman. This seems to contradict other passages in the Old Testament, which report that Moses was a gifted orator and leader. Moses, you may remember, spent the first forty years of his life as a privileged member of the Egyptian royal court; he was found by Pharaoh's daughter in the reeds along the bank of the Nile, where he had been hidden to prevent his being slain along with other male infants doomed by Pharaoh's edict.

When Moses went to Pharaoh to demand the release of the Israelites, Aaron accompanied him. According to Exodus, it was Aaron, not Moses, who cast down his staff, which changed into a serpent and gobbled up the enchantments of Pharaoh's magicians.

Like Moses, Aaron was not allowed by God to enter the Promised Land at the end of the forty years in the wilderness. After surrendering his priestly robes to his son Eleazar, Aaron died at age 123 and was buried on Mount Hor. That, at least, is according to Numbers 33. Deuteronomy 10 says Aaron was buried at Mosera. In either case, no mention of the Staff is given—was it buried with Aaron, was it handed to Eleazar, or did it continue to be carried in the Ark of the Covenant?

I have dealt primarily with the Christian version of the story, as related by tradition and the ubiquitous King James Version of the Bible. The reason, of course, is not because of some personal bias, but because this would be the predominant cultural and literary tradition for Indiana Jones. It should be remembered, however, that Moses and his siblings are important figures in Islam as well as Judaism and Christianity. Also, the story of Moses achieved special resonance when Israel was once again declared an independent nation on May 14, 1948.

The Omega Book

Although the Omega Book is a product of my imagination, it was inspired by an ancient and nearly universal belief: that somewhere, perhaps in the shadowy area between this world and the next, there exists a carefully kept and all-knowing record of our lives. This myth, in one form or another, seems to have been around for as long as we have. It is a myth, as Joseph Campbell once described myth, not because it is a lie, but because it represents a metaphorical—or, more accurately, the penultimate—truth. "Penultimate," Campbell said, because ultimate truth is beyond words and images.

In Christianity, the Book of Life is the record of all of those who have been redeemed by Jesus Christ and who will therefore be allowed to enter the New Jerusalem, as described in Revelation. Three books with similar titles are traditionally evaluated on Rosh Hashanah, the Jewish New Year: The Book of Life of the Wicked, The Book of Life of the Righteous, and The Book of Life of "Those in Between." The righteous are promised a good and eternal life, while the wicked are immediately condemned to death. Judgment of those in between—and I presume most would fall into this category—is deferred until Yom Kippur.

Other religions have had similar beliefs, and they go at least as far back as Babylon, where the gods could erase the names of the wicked from "The Tablets of Destiny" and enter them instead onto "The Tablets of Transgression."

The title of *my* book comes from the last character of the Greek alphabet, which resonates with biblical finality; it was also influenced by physicist Frank J. Tipler's controversial "Omega Point" theory. In brief, Tipler suggests that the universe might evolve into a kind of all-knowing and all-powerful computer at the end of time and simulate "an entire visible universe for the personal use of each and every human" who ever lived. The result? Virtual resurrection. Although Tipler's theory, which includes a discussion of how much computing power would be needed for these worlds without end, is thought-provoking and well-argued, it seems to me that it is just the latest incarnation of an old belief. But instead of being represented by a book, which was the most powerful information storage device in the time of Moses, the Omega Point uses a computer, which prepares to launch the myth into the twenty-first century. The ultimate truth may lurk in the wordless areas of our psyches, where there is transcendent truth and an unending tally of our own good and evil.

The Sphinx

Through tradition, the Great Sphinx at Giza has long been the symbol of unfathomable mysteries. The name "sphinx" is Greek for an imaginary and evil monster with the head of a woman and the winged body of a lion that was prone to destroy travelers who could not supply the correct answer to her riddles; the most famous of all Greek sphinxes appears in the story of Oedipus. Egyptian sphinxes are similar, but could have a human or animal head.

In mythology, all sphinxes seem to be connected with riddles or ancient secrets, with terror following close behind. And in literature, sphinxes have also been used to represent future horrors. In the H. G. Wells classic *The Time Machine,* for example, the dreaded Morlocks emerge from their subterranean chambers through a Sphinx-like structure to feast upon the childlike Eloi.

Recently, the age of the Great Sphinx at Giza and its significance to world culture has been the subject of several popular books and television shows that have traditional Egyptologists spinning. In *The Message of the Sphinx,* for example, Graham Hancock and Robert Bauval argue that the enigmatic monument was not built around 2500 B.C., as Egyptologists believe, but some ten thousand years earlier.

The authors cite the work of John West, who believes that the deep erosion on the Sphinx and the surrounding enclosure were caused not by wind and sand, but by water. The weathering, West says, must have taken place before the breakup of the last Ice Age—which, to say the least, would upset the conventional wisdom about the emergence of civilization.

Hancock and Bauval believe the Sphinx was created not by the Egyptians, but by an earlier and technologically superior civilization. It is not a new idea, and there is a long tradition that the Sphinx is a monument created by an advanced and now-lost civilization before the biblical flood. Edgar Cayce, the "sleeping prophet," predicted that the lost records of Atlantis would be found beneath the paws of the Sphinx. This Hall of Records, Cayce said, would be rediscovered at or near the end of the twentieth century.

Authors Hancock and Bauval seem to agree, and they steep themselves in detailed facts and figures and conjecture about the Great Sphinx in much the same way that pyramidologists have done for generations.

"There is something of momentous importance there," they write, "waiting to be found—by seismic surveys, by drilling and excavation, in short by a rediscovery and exploration of the hidden corridors and chambers (beneath the Sphinx). . . . It could be the ultimate prize."

Cayce, by the way, believed that he was the reincarnation of an Atlantean prince named Ra-Ta.

Dr. Mark Lehner, the world's foremost expert on the Sphinx, is also traditional Egyptology's foremost and perhaps most eloquent spokesman. In a letter to Hancock and Bauval after reading portions of the manuscript of *The Message of the Sphinx,* Lehner wrote:

"I began to suggest to the Cayce community that they look at the Egypt/Atlantis story as a myth in the sense that Joseph Campbell popularized, or that Carl Jung drew upon in his psychology of archetypes. Although the myth is not *literally true,* it may in some way be literally *true.* The Cayce 'readings' themselves say, in their own way, that the inner world of symbols and archetypes is more 'real' than the particulars of the physical world. I compared Cayce's Hall of Records to the Wizard of Oz. Yes, we all want the 'sound and the fury' and powerful wizardry to be real, without having to pay any attention to the little man behind the curtain (ourselves). In archaeology, many dilettantes and New Agers want to be on the trail of a lost civilization, aliens, yes, 'the gods,' without having to pay attention to the real people behind time's curtain and without having to deal with the difficult subject matter upon which so-called 'orthodox' scholars base their views."

In one of the ironies with which archaeology is rife, it should be noted that Lehner—the orthodox world's expert—began his study of the Sphinx because he was inspired by Cayce's prophecy, and with the backing of an organization of Cayce believers. But, Lehner says, the more he studied the more he came to believe in empirical evidence over prophecy.

A Final Note

This series of original Indiana Jones adventures would not have been possible, of course, without the wonderful characters and situations that *Raiders of the Lost Ark* gave us. Thanks to moviemakers George Lucas and Steven Spielberg for worlds of entertainment, and to all of the actors in the Indiana Jones trilogy for helping to create such easily identifiable characters. One cannot write about Indy— or, I suspect, read about him—without imagining Harrison Ford.

Thanks are especially due to my long-suffering editor at Bantam, Tom Dupree, who shepherded the first three books to publication, and to his successor, Pat Lobrutto, who suffered less only because he had just one of my books to worry about; to my agent, Robin Rue, for her belief and support; and to my Austin friend Fred Bean, for his creative contributions. Special recognition is also deserved by the late Gene DeGruson, special collections librarian at Pittsburg State University in Kansas, whose unselfish contributions enriched these and many other books.

There are many others I should thank, including librarians and researchers across the country, but unfortunately the list is too long to cite each individual. A collective thanks to all must suffice.

That said, I pass the hat and whip.

ABOUT THE AUTHOR

MAX McCOY is an award-winning journalist and author whose Bantam novels include *The Sixth Rider* and *Sons of Fire*. He lives in Pittsburg, Kansas.